UNTETHERED

Philippa Holloway is a writer and academic with a varied career history that includes being a goatherd, a medical technician at a racing circuit, and a library assistant. Her short fiction has been published internationally, and her debut novel *The Half-life of Snails* was longlisted for the RSL Ondaatje prize. It has also been featured in an international podcast, serialised in a national newspaper, and praised on BBC Radio 4's *Front Row* programme.

UNTETHERED

Philippa Holloway

PARTHIAN

Parthian, Cardigan SA43 1ED
www.parthianbooks.com
© Philippa Holloway
ISBN: 978-1-914595-85-1
Editor: Carly Holmes
Cover Design: Syncopated Pandemonium
Typeset by Elaine Sharples
Printed by 4edge Limited
Published with the financial support of the Books Council of Wales
British Library Cataloguing in Publication Data
A cataloguing record for this book is available from the British Library.
Printed on FSC accredited paper

For my dad, who taught me about good wine, fine whisky,
and from whom I inherited my wicked sense of humour.
You loved bird watching so much,
sorry I killed so many of them in this book…

CONTENTS

A CLOUD OF STARLINGS	1
BEACHED	20
UN/DETERMINED	24
A SUDDEN RUSH OF AIR	41
ANOTHER PLACE	60
NO COMMENT	75
HANDPRINTS	91
HOMING	100
SEVEN TEETH	118
THE WEIGHT OF A SHOE	127
THE MESSAGE	140
ACKNOWLEDGEMENTS	155

A CLOUD OF STARLINGS

She is almost home when she sees them, senses them first. It is dusk, the sun just gone below the stone wall of the top field, and she is easing the car between tight hedgerows when there is a faint crunch beneath the tyres, felt more than heard. She drops to a lower gear, slows and searches the road with tired eyes.

There are dark shapes, lumpen and irregular, scattered in the lane.

She stops, unease pooling in her gut, glances around at the darkening fields, grey sheep drifting beyond the wire fence and bare hawthorn branches, then back at the patch of road illuminated by her headlights, as if the scattering might have vanished. But no, there are dead birds littering the lane, and if she drives on, she will crush them beneath the wheels of her car.

She is only a few hundred metres from home, can see the dark shape of their farmhouse on her right, the warm beacon of light from the kitchen window. Today was her day to work, a long shift at the hospital, paperwork piled on the passenger seat, and her husband is cooking dinner somewhere beyond these tiny wind-ruffled corpses. She wants the warmth of her hall to envelop her, the glass of wine he'll pour when he hears her car pull up, the embrace of her daughter like a fierce rugby tackle hitting her side before she even has time to slip off her shoes and stash them on the rack.

She wants routine.

She eases the car forward, trying to steer around the bodies, and feeling her failure through the tyres. As she reaches the apex of the curved lane, she stops again. There are too many. Hundreds, perhaps. The headlights pick out the branches of the raggedy hawthorn in sharp grey spikes and there are more birds caught there, suspended in the bare twigs, heads lolling. It's as if an entire flock has fallen from the sky.

She can't bear to drive over them, kills the engine instead and fills her arms with the files, her heavy bag tugging her shoulder. The wind flutters the pages in her arms, threatening to tear them loose and release them into the air, and her hair whips into her mouth, cuts her vision. She picks her way through the dead birds, careful not to tread on their wing tips or curled toes. A macabre hopscotch.

In the porch she struggles with her load, manages to turn the key in the lock and tumbles into the hallway. She can hear the radio on in the kitchen, but no child rushes for her waist, and no one calls out a greeting. She dumps the folders on the sideboard and walks through into the kitchen. Dan is leaning over the stove, sniffing the steam rising from a cassoulet pan.

'Where's Sophie?' she asks.

'Christ, Siân! You made me jump!' He replaces the lid and rests his hand on his chest, right where his heart is now racing. 'I didn't hear you get back.'

'I had to leave the car in the lane. Have you seen the birds?' She goes to the fridge, takes out a half-empty bottle of wine and pours a glass. It doesn't taste as good as last night, a sour aftertaste near the back of her tongue.

'Yeah, we found them on the way home from school.'

'And you didn't think to clear the path?'

'The police told us not to. They want to send someone round, find out what's going on.'

'You called the police?'

'Yeah, of course. You don't think it's weird?'

'Of course it's weird, but is it really a police matter?'

'Well, who else would you call?'

She thinks for a moment, unsure. Who do you call when birds start falling from the sky? She walks over to the back window, to where the sun has slipped behind the horizon and the floodlights from the nuclear power station are competing with the sunset. It isn't close, but close enough. A low, sandcastle-shaped block just over a mile away. No, if it were that there would have been alarms, evacuations.

'I have no idea,' she says, and takes a gulp of the wine. 'So, when can we clear the road?'

'Tomorrow sometime.'

Tomorrow it is his turn to work: twelve hours on the road in his green uniform, waiting in laybys for a heart attack or RTA to fill his time. Half the time he's bored, half the time so busy his shifts run over by four or seven hours at a stretch.

Siân wanders through to the lounge, sees Sophie hunched over the dining table. A skinny girl, just turned twelve. Small for her age and still in pigtails and baggy jeans. Siân walks over, expecting to see homework, but finds her adding to extensive notes in an A4 sketchbook, the opposite page filled with a detailed study of a bird's face and feather patterns. One word is bolder than the others, as if she's pressed too hard with the pencil. WHY?

'What are you doing, Sophs?'

'Research.' She doesn't look up, doesn't squeeze her eyes

shut against her mother's chest as if she wished she were still small, carriable.

Siân stands behind her daughter, admiring the delicate tracing of the feather patterns, the perfectly proportioned head and beak. 'Did you copy it?'

'I took photos.' Sophie swipes her finger across her phone and the screen is filled with the stark image of a dead bird, head lolling just as in the drawing, claws curled closed. Its chest is petrol green and speckled. A starling. Her daughter glances up, as if for approval, but with worry shimmering in a fine line beneath her eyes.

'It's a brilliant sketch, Sophs.'

Sophie almost replies, but is cut off.

'Dinner is nearly ready!' Dan's head peeking round the door. 'Time to pack up, okay? Siân, can you set the table?'

Sophie carefully closes the book, replaces her pencils in their tin one by one and in order of hardness; 2H, H, F, HB, B…

Despite the hearty stew ladled onto her plate, and the hours that have dragged since lunchtime, Siân's appetite is compromised. The chicken, so tender it slides off the bone, reminds her too much of the soft crush beneath her tyres. She picks at the carrots instead, spearing them from the stock with her fork.

'Good day at school?'

Sophie is quiet, similarly averse to eating her meat. She doesn't eat much anyway, so this isn't unusual. She shrugs, avoiding the question. Siân and Dan exchange a glance. She's struggling to make friends, despite the move to a better school, one that can support her needs. One without bullies, they hope.

'Did you have science today?' Her favourite subject, that she hopes will lead to a medical career like her parents. She doesn't know yet, thinks Siân, what a brutal route that is.

'Why do you think they died, Mum?'

'Let's not talk about it at the dinner table, huh?'

'But...'

'Let's not.'

And yet none of them can think of anything else all evening.

'I've got a migraine.'

Sophie is still under the duvet, refusing to get up and dressed for school. Siân kneels beside the bed.

'I know it's difficult, sweetheart. I know. But you need to go in. The more you go, the easier it will be.'

'But my head hurts. My eyes hurt. My stomach is sick.'

Siân lays her hand on her child's forehead as if this might tell her what the matter is. Eleven years of training and specialising, and when it's her own daughter she resorts to a palm on the face. She's convinced the symptoms are fake, but not convinced enough to force her to get dressed, eat breakfast and then walk past the scene in the lane. If she stays home they can both avoid it, watch TV all day, pretend nothing is the matter.

'You're not faking?'

'I promise, Mummy. It hurts when I move my head.'

'Okay. I'll get painkillers, you stay there. No phone though, if your head is bad. It'll only make it worse.'

Sophie scowls but knows she can't argue. Siân goes to the kitchen, her daughter's phone in one hand. She runs the tap for cold water and gets distracted by the searches her child has made on the smartphone's browser.

Murmuration.

Curse.

Radiation.

Meaning of dead birds.

Electromagnetic pulse.

How to dissect a bird.

Diseases in starlings.

The times are listed too: 11.58pm, 12.14am, the last one at 2.32am. No wonder she is tired and headachy. She takes the paracetamol tablets upstairs and watches Sophie swallow them easily, suppresses a vague melancholy when the memory of sticky pink Calpol surfaces, a nostalgia for teething fevers and chickenpox and all those manageable traumas that can be soothed away with strawberry flavours and cuddles.

'Will you be okay if I go down and do some work?'

Sophie nods, eyelids heavy. The room is stuffy and hot. She'll be back to sleep soon, Siân thinks.

Two hours later, the kitchen is sparkling clean and there is paperwork covering the desk in Siân's study. She has almost forgotten her daughter, upstairs, sleeping, as she peer-reviews an article on how to manage parental expectations in cases of childhood brain tumours. She has read the line *many parents will struggle to align expectations of their child's pre-illness perceived futures with the reality of their new disabilities and needs* at least six times, stuck on a loop of self-reflection. What was she expecting when Sophie was born? She knows she tried hard not to imagine, not to build a picture of a fantasy family that might never come to fruition. They've been lucky, haven't they? Sophie has suffered none of the terrible physical illnesses she herself has seen decimate families before her eyes. But her daughter isn't what she expected, and now that this thought has been released it can't be caught again.

A flash of movement catches her eye, through the window. A white van glimpsed through hedges as it navigates the lane. She is grateful for the distraction, despite dreading their arrival all morning. She lays the article carefully on the desk so she won't lose her place, and fetches her coat and wellies, ready to talk to the police, to face the carnage at the boundary of her garden.

It's sunny, clear and cold, and she keeps her hands in her pockets as she walks down the lane, standing at one end of the tideline of bodies while the van disperses three people, their ages and genders hidden by white hooded cover-alls and blue plastic booties, at the other side. She waves, calls a greeting that seems inappropriately cheerful under the circumstances, as if she is hailing the milk delivery or postie.

One of the people starts to navigate a path through towards her, like a space explorer walking on alien land; arms and legs thick puffy white, shapeless feet lifted unnaturally high, gait unnaturally slow. Siân shuffles her feet, begins to worry about her own attire. Are they wearing the forensic suits to protect the scene or themselves? She starts to walk towards them, as if meeting in the middle will somehow negate the threat, share out the unpleasantness between them, but the person in the suit holds up a hand, calls through their mask, 'No, stay there. I'll come to you.'

When they arrive at her side the person pulls down their mask, smiles. A woman, taller than Siân and with soft crinkles around her eyes that immediately soothe.

'So, what the heck happened here?' she asks.

'I thought it was your job to tell us.'

'A joint effort, probably. Are you Siân Evans?'

Siân nods.

'DC Sally Winters, from the Rural Crime Unit.'

The other two people are already photographing the scene, one kneeling for close-ups on the ground, the other taking a wide shot before focussing on the birds caught in the hedge spikes and wire fence. Siân turns briefly to glance at the house, catches sight of her daughter like a pale ghost haunting the window. Big round eyes that give her an alien visage. It takes Siân a moment to realise Sophie is using binoculars, studying the scene. It takes another few moments for her to realise she is secretly wishing her child was at school, playing video games, watching trash on TV like a normal pre-teen rather than obsessing over the birds in the lane. The thoughts crowd and split, disperse and settle somewhere out of sight as the woman starts asking questions.

'When did this happen, then?' Winters has a small digital voice-recorder in her outstretched hand.

'Don't you need my ID or something, first? To record our details?'

'Nope, it was all logged last night. You are Mrs Evans? This is your property?'

She has sowed the seeds of doubt, corrects it. 'Yes, sorry. And I don't know exactly. I was at work, didn't get home until... maybe ten to six? It was already dark, or almost dark.'

'Did anyone else see what happened?'

'Wasn't that logged last night?' She is trying to keep the edge off her voice, but is frustrated with the pace so far, wants to go back inside and get Sophie away from the window. 'Sorry. No, my husband found them when he got back from the school run, at about four o'clock. He'd been shopping beforehand, left the house at maybe two-ish? There was nothing there then.'

'Did he tell you if he saw anything unusual before he left? The birds moving oddly? Any strange smells? A predator, maybe?'

'What kind of predator?' Siân's heart leaps involuntarily, images of panthers or skulking teens with pellet guns lurking in the ditches or behind the old stone walls near the bottom field. Faceless and fearless.

'Birds of prey?'

'There's a pair of sparrowhawks that nest nearby. But how—'

'Hello!' The woman is looking past Siân, smiling.

Sophie is standing in the lane, jeans and wellies on under her nightdress, her heavy winter coat open and flapping in the breeze.

'Sophs! Go back in!'

Sophie comes closer, unusually defiant. Stands right at the tideline of bodies, her face serious, a question dimpling her brow. She slips a skinny hand into Siân's and watches as the other two investigators start taking samples of soil and holding strips of reactive paper in the air before sealing them into plastic tubes.

'Not at school today?' the woman asks Sophie, pulling her hood off.

'I'm ill.'

'Ill?' This question directed at Siân, a hard undertone.

'I'd better get her back indoors, do you need anything else?'

'I'll follow you up in a minute, just to check what her symptoms are, if that's okay?'

'Of course. I'll put the kettle on.' She squeezes Sophie's hand perhaps a little too tightly as she leads her back to the house. The tech-induced headache will now be logged, taken into account. Evidence. She knows because she herself has picked out the tiniest clue in her patients' conversations, grasped at every route to causality and diagnosis so many times. She can't fault the investigator; just hopes she is being over cautious. Sophie is fine, nothing wrong with her at all.

In the sky between her and the sea a murmuration of starlings spins and dives, but Siân doesn't notice. She is too busy trying not to think.

By late afternoon the lane is clear. Siân couldn't wait until Dan got home, couldn't rely on him finishing on time or having the energy to sweep and bag the birds even if he did. She hoped the police would remove them, but when she asked, they just shrugged and replied that they didn't have the facilities. They took just five bodies, each sealed in individual plastic bags and packed inside the kind of insulated container that is used to transport organs or picnics. Siân stood in the lane and watched them leave, fury building at the mess at her feet as the white van flashed in and out of sight between the hedgerows then vanished beyond the copse near the junction. She'd left it for a while, drinking tea in her study, trying to read the rest of the paper. *Sometimes the death of an afflicted child is a relief for parents of multiple children, as it signals a return to a familial routine more culturally accepted as normative. For those with only one child, however, it can trigger feelings of failure and remorse, during which the expectations of normative life from before diagnosis are reignited…*

When she did go out, with a garden broom and shovel, a wheelbarrow, she covered her mouth with a scarf and wore thick gardening gloves. Picked those caught in the hedgerow carefully, as if they were wilting autumn flowers. Hardened herself to the smear and scrape as she cleared the lane, heaped the birds and wheeled them down to the boundary ditch. She piled them high, tossed in dry logs from the pile that fed their log burner, and stood back while the pyre burned. Smoke twisting and swirling, dark against the clear winter sky. Once the fire was dampened, she stripped in the kitchen, piled her clothes in the washing machine and spent over half an hour beneath the hot spray of the shower, washing her hair three times to get the smell of smoke and burnt feathers out.

She knows she should go back to her study, finish the paper

and close the file before dinner. But she remembers her promise, her first plan – afternoon TV, chocolate treats, cuddles – an easy way for them to forget the trauma of the night before and this morning. Dan might be home in time for a late supper. She can do Sophie a pizza, send her to bed early and then cook something special. Open a fresh bottle. Back to routine.

She turns on the TV in the lounge and goes to look for her daughter, expecting to find her in her bedroom with a book, or drawing something detailed and far too advanced for her age in one of her sketchbooks, but her room is empty. She walks through the house calling, checks the bedrooms and kitchen, checks the lounge again in case Sophie was in there, curled in a corner somewhere and so quiet maybe Siân missed her when she drifted through earlier. She is just beginning to panic, her mind in a contiguous state of denial and worry, when she thinks to check the garden.

Siân pushes open the door at the rear of the house. Out here there is a large sunroom, sheltered from the wind by glazed panels, a view across the garden and fields and towards the coast. The nuclear power station hunkers half-hidden behind tall conifers on the edge of the view. Sophie is there, the table where they eat summer suppers covered with newspaper sheets, three dead birds laid out in a row. She is wearing Perspex goggles from an old toy chemistry set, blue nitrile gloves and a plastic apron almost certainly taken from Siân's study or Dan's paramedic bag. She is holding a small paring knife, the sharpest knife in the house, and just as Siân steps onto the decking makes a clean incision down the breast of the first bird.

Siân bites her tongue, doesn't want to cry out or shout in

case her daughter's hand – small and skinny inside those baggy blue gloves – slips and slices her own flesh open. She stands mesmerised as the child uses her thumbs to prise open the chest walls of the bird, opening it like a tiny biological book, muttering something under her breath. An incantation or self-reassurance, Siân can't quite tell. Either way it raises the hairs on her arms and makes her heart flutter. This is an unnatural juxtaposition of work and home, her daughter the fulcrum of the uncanny balance. Sophie pauses, peering inside the thorax, then checks the information on the iPad next to her.

If she closes her eyes, takes only the outline of her child into her head, Siân can imagine her daughter is painting, or crafting something innocent and colourful out of playdough or clay. Can sink into the pastel-coloured memories of the expectations she carried along with the bump of her pregnancy. But when she opens them again her daughter is pulling out the entrails of a dead starling. Siân watches as she begins removing organs, sealing them in small plastic food bags and weighing them on the digital kitchen scales, noting down the details in her sketchbook. She is fascinated by her child's apparent calm: this child who cried for a month when they hit a hare on the road to Abersoch one balmy summer's evening, who can't watch adverts appealing for animal charities, or throw away a stuffed toy. This child who struggles to make friends, to make eye contact, to walk without tripping, is suddenly an elegant surgeon, half-woman, precise.

Siân shuffles closer, letting her presence be known. Bites back her instinct to gather the corpses into the newspaper and throw them out. Instead, she moves and sits opposite, waits for Sophie to speak.

'Are you mad at me?' The gloved hand shaking slightly, the knife poised over the emptied torso.

'No, baby. But what are you doing?'

'An autopsy.'

'Why?'

'Because I need to know.' Her eyes are wide behind the goggles, her shoulders tight. 'Will you help me?'

Siân pauses, for no more than a second or two, but it's enough for disappointment to cloud Sophie's eyes. She looks down at the dead bird, tears welling.

'No. I think you're doing a perfectly good job yourself. But I'll sit with you and answer any questions you may have.'

The eyes flash back up, a half-smile flickering. 'Really?'

'Of course. Now, what have you found so far?'

'Everything inside is normal. And the wing-patterns aren't messed up, like the ones after the Sher... Char...'

'Chornobyl disaster?'

'Yes.'

Neither of them glance out of the windows. Siân tries not to let the molten burn of self-criticism show in her face. How does her daughter know these things? There are filters on their internet settings: no violence, no porn. She always expected those two to be the biggest threat. But science and history contain both, she realises. What has her daughter read? How many times has Siân let her down?

'Anything else?'

'There is blood on their nostrils, every one of them. And their necks are really floppy, but I don't know if it's just because they are dead or if they are broken.'

Siân slips on a spare pair of gloves and carefully feels down the spine of a bird, from its eggshell-thin skull to its delicately ridged hips, returns to the neck and locates the fault.

'Let me feel that one.'

Sophie hands over another bird, and Siân finds the same fault, in a similar place. She considers lying, feigning ignorance, but can't decide what benefit there would be. Would not knowing that both birds have broken necks actually help her daughter any more than finding out the truth?

'Well?'

'Here.' Siân hands one bird back and guides her daughter's sheathed hands into place, talks her through the exam. Watches as her daughter finds the loose connection in the bird's beaded spine. A smile of triumph, a frown of thought.

'Both of them?'

Siân nods.

'All of them?'

Siân shrugs. 'Maybe. We'll have to wait and see what the experts think.'

Sophie nods, satisfied for now, and together they clear the table, wrapping each bird carefully in newspaper and laying them on the back step while they wash the knife and scales, disinfect the table. Before they remove and dispose of the gloves and apron, they bury the birds in a shallow grave in the neglected flower border, and Sophie marks the spot with a smooth, rain-polished stone. As they finish, a huge murmuration of starlings rises into the sky a few fields away, twisting like smoke, darkening with density and then dispersing. They watch for a while, entranced, disturbed, and Sophie's hand creeps into Siân's, clings tight.

'I used to think that was beautiful,' she whispers, 'but now

I just think it's frightening. Like they are going to turn and swoop down on me.'

Siân squeezes back.

'They'd never do that. They're just flying, having fun or hunting flies. Let's go and eat chocolate and watch TV, hey?' And they turn their backs on the birds and go into the creamy warmth of the lounge, where they both pretend to enjoy the film despite neither of them caring at all what happens.

A week later the phone rings. Sophie is in the bath, Dan cooking, so Siân answers.

'Mrs Evans?'

'Speaking.'

'It's Sally Winters, from the forensic team? We came out last week to investigate the sudden death of a flock of birds on your property?'

'Yes.' Siân's heartrate picks up a notch, fearing a bad toxicology report, news of a radiation leak from the power station across the fields, warnings about new predators in the area.

'Well, our investigations have found nothing suspect or worrying at all, it seems the birds died from blunt force trauma, and considering the scale of the incident we conclude this was caused by them flying into the ground at speed.'

'Flying into the ground? Why would they do that?'

'We can't know for sure, but occasionally birds in large flocks get confused—'

'Confused? Birds don't just get confused and fly into the

floor!' Her voice is rising, and she checks it, tries to hush in case Sophie hears.

'I understand your concern, Mrs Evans, but there have been previous cases, not in the UK, but elsewhere, that have shown that, very rarely, when startled by something like a hawk or predatory bird and trying to perform evasive manoeuvres, they fail to pull up in time and fatalities can occur. These birds were distracted, travelling too fast. They made a mistake.'

But nature doesn't make mistakes like that, surely? Siân thinks. It's humans who miscalculate, who slip up, who say the wrong thing in a consultation with the parents or push the scalpel in a fraction of an inch too far... nature is far more carefully programmed, instincts honed and in tune with the rest of the planet. Birds don't fly into things because they aren't using their judgement, they are just... flying.

'Are you still there, Mrs Evans?'

'Yes, thank you for letting me know... I'm relieved it's not...'

'No problem, take care.'

And the line clicks dead.

Sophie is calling for help, for someone to hold the showerhead over her while she rinses the conditioner out of her long hair. Siân takes the stairs slowly, words from the article she still hasn't finished reviewing coming back to her mind in flits and starts: *Practitioners must be aware that parents of terminally ill children will always seek answers, even when there are none to give...*

'Who was it, Mum?' Sophie's skin is deep pink where the hot water has caused the blood to rush to the surface. She sits with one arm folded around her knees, her budding chest covered. She is twirling a wet lock of dark hair around her finger, studying the split ends. She hates hairdressers, can't abide the tickle and tug of a cut.

'It was the police, calling about the birds.'

Her finger stops, her attention caught. She waits, not quite breathless.

'It was an accident. They said the birds just flew into the ground.'

Sophie pauses to think it over.

'No. Tell me what really happened.'

'That's what happened, Sophie. And if you think about it, that's what our findings indicated too.'

'But birds can't just fly at the floor, they'd move!'

They may even seek to blame medical personnel on whom they have placed unrealistic and/or unexpected expectations of power. While they might know the situation is beyond the control of medical staff, they may still harbour fantasies that their child will be 'the miracle' among the masses.

'They made a mistake, baby.'

'No, there must be a better reason, a real reason. Like magnetism, or a seismic tremor too low for us to detect.' Sophie's voice is thin in the steam from the bath. Desperate.

'Sometimes there isn't an answer, Sophie, sometimes nature just... makes mistakes.'

Sophie looks at the taps, at her own distorted reflection.

'Like me?' she whispers.

'What do you mean?' But Siân already knows. Sophie is quite old enough to notice she isn't like the other children at her school, or the last school.

'Freaks, like me?'

Siân kneels and lifts the shower head off its cradle at the edge of the bath, runs the water until it's warm.

'You're not a "freak", Sophs. You're just... special.'

'Special, as in "wrong". As in "weird". As in "don't be her friend, it might be catching".' Her face is buried in her knees. Siân has no idea what to say, never had any trouble at school herself. Always thought that Sophie would be the same as her, in miniature, with maybe Dan's nose or eyes, or sense of humour... but that she'd be recognisable in more than just her shape and form. Her daughter is a wet, lanky ball of tears. Lonely, unsure, and all Siân can do for a minute is hold the spray of water over her head and smooth the creamy conditioner out until the hair squeaks as she rubs her hand through it.

She stands and fetches a towel off the rail, wraps it around her child, and pulls her in tight for a hug.

If there is too much of a gap between expectations and reality, and parents struggle to adjust in time, there may need to be a referral to professional services for counselling and/or family therapy.

Siân takes her daughter's shoulders and stares her straight in her eyes, remembering the calm hand with the paring knife, the face beneath the goggles. She sees the woman her daughter could become.

'Special as in "smarter", as in "better than I ever hoped".'

Sophie holds her gaze, but Siân never wavers. In the field behind the house a murmuration of starlings lifts up, swirls, and settles, quiet for now.

BEACHED

How do you pick up an octopus?

The sand is wet, concrete hard, the rippled ridges from the outgoing tide stiff enough to turn an ankle. Miles of it stretching out either side and the grey water retreating towards a steel horizon, and I'm alone with salt wind in my eyes. The question surfaces without expectation of an answer. It's a question for me, barely whispered.

The octopus is a huge orange tangle a few feet beyond the lapping water. Already the gulls are circling.

The dog approaches again, creeps in, sniffs, cannot file the smell as anything other than alien and therefore a threat, and jumps back again. A yap or two, shouting *danger! danger!* Then he's distracted by the gulls and gallops off.

I stand still, staring at the octopus, at its deflated mantle and the two golf-ball eyes closed aside its head, the inert swirl of its tentacles, silted and mucky. The tide is going out, and with it the chances of survival. I crouch, can see the saltwater draining from the sand, the sun and wind already making dust of the peaks. It's drying out. Its rubber skin will harden, and any spark of life will be snuffed by the sunshine.

But how do you pick up an octopus?

I get up, circle it, try to gauge its size. If it were tiny, I could cup it in my palms and take it a few steps to the waves. I'd even wade in deep, let my shoes fill up and jeans become sodden to give it a chance, to see it bloom and flex in the water. But this beast is too big for cupped hands, too big for arms even. Each leg, I guess, is four or five feet long if unknotted and stretched, the head and mantle the size of a floor cushion. I walk around it, stepping carefully so as not to tread on a suckered tip.

Alone, even if I could bear its weight, I could not contain its form. It would slip, tipping through a gap in my grasp, between elbow and armpit maybe, weight shifting. Any attempt to contain one limb would cause another to slide free, slapping my ankles, tripping me. And that's if it doesn't move.

I scan the beach again for someone to share the responsibility. If I had walked the other way, if I had thought the orange mass to be rubbish, a nest of fishing line or a stranded buoy and ropes, I'd have walked right past at a distance and this would not be my problem. But now it is. I'm snagged by the situation, culpable if I leave.

There is no one else close enough to summon. A lone walker has appeared about half a mile or more upwind, their dog also chasing gulls, but when I stand and wave like a mad thing, like one of the offshore wind turbines on the horizon with arms wheeling in the wind, they don't even wave back. They are walking away, getting smaller, and this creature at my feet is demanding attention.

I stride away a few paces to see how it feels to leave it, and my stomach cramps. My mouth fills with saliva and bitter guilt. My brain races with images of wheelbarrows, of wet blankets and a team of people in polo-shirts with a charity logo emblazoned on the breast. Something reassuring, like a leaping dolphin, cartoonish and smiling. I pull out my phone and start scrolling for animal rescue charities, sea-life centres, and the signal dips and disappears, comes back again and then flits away. I walk further off, and my chest tightens. Thumbing the screen, the dog dancing around my ankles. It's Sunday. I click on a link and hear two distant rings, then the signal cuts again.

All of this might be a waste, I realise, if the octopus is already dead. I stand on a teetering branch of driftwood and lift my phone high, ask it with chilled fingers how to tell if an octopus is dead, and sunlight dazzles me. A headline on the search says it could survive for up to sixty minutes out of water, but the page won't load. It must be twenty minutes or more already.

Back at its side I crouch and reach out a tentative finger, touch the jelly head and seek out signs of movements, of breathing. It flinches. The sea has retreated further away, and I'm running out of time, but can't just walk away. No. In the quivering sides and gentle coil of it, there is life, and I'm as trapped here as it is.

I wonder if I can drag it, shudder at the thought of a leg stretching and snapping, a noise that could only be a scream, or that maybe only the dog could hear, but that I'd feel through its skin. But I have to do something, at least until someone else comes along and I can trap them here with me, demand they assist.

I crouch and start to dig. Make a moat around it at first, then push my hands deeper underneath to make a pool. The water seeps in as the creature sinks, and my back aches with the effort. I kneel and soak my jeans, but keep digging, until I'm lying down and my shoulder is pressed into the sand, both arms underneath the cold wet rubber of it. I can feel its weight, and the tentacles curl and respond. We are both in this pit, but at least it's buying some time. I slither out, stand up and stand back. I am thirsty and sore and my eyes sting with frustration, but I still can't leave. I know the water will drain away as the tide retreats.

So I do the only thing left. I walk to the waves and cup my hands, carry the trickling gift back to the pool, and pour. Back and forth, waiting for the tide to turn.

UN/DETERMINED

You are still being stitched up when the doctor comes back in. By now, all embarrassment at being seen with your legs apart and insides exposed has waned to a distant echo of shame that hovers somewhere behind your throat, like the first sign of a cold. The doctor stands beside the bed and coughs to get your full attention, but when you look up into his plump, childish face he is staring hard at his paperwork, fingering his ear with his pinkie.

'Yes?'

Your voice has a surreal quality to it, sharpened by an involuntary wince as the needle nicks raw flesh, hoarsened by the guttural shouts from an hour before. You barely recognise it. You are a different person now.

The doctor glances at you briefly, then walks to stand over the plastic cot.

'Have you announced the news?'

'No, I've been kinda busy.' You gesture to the midwife hunkered between your legs, trying to inject some humour into the situation. He doesn't smile.

'Good.' He pauses. 'I wouldn't.'

'Wouldn't what?'

'Announce the birth. Not yet, anyway. We need to do some more tests first, we should have an answer for you in a week or so.' He nods, as if to convince himself, and turns to leave.

'Wait!'

He twists at the door, eyes flitting between the window and a point somewhere beside your head.

'Does it matter?'

'Most people still think so,' he shrugs. 'Your call.'

The midwife is finished, signs off with a flourish of 'There we go!' and a snap of the scissors, easing your legs out of the stirrups. She presses a thick cotton sanitary towel against the sore stitches and covers you with the blanket. Doors open and swing closed. The doctor is gone but Mark is back, shuffling from foot to foot and rubbing his scratchy, stubbly chin to hide a yawn as he waits for the midwife to move out of the way. Now she is bending over the plastic crib, inspecting the contents as someone would inspect leftovers, trying to determine their freshness. She wiggles a finger in front of the screwed-up face and speaks in the silly kind of voice people reserve for infants and animals. 'I always think babies look like George W. Bush for the first few days.' She carries on staring, as you feel a flush of indignation spread across your chest and colour your throat. Her voice changes back to adult speak. 'Churchill, it used to be. A pickled Churchill. But I think Bush. Confused, you know? A bit boss-eyed. Girl or boy?'

She hasn't read the notes. She wasn't at the birth. At least, you don't think so – the similarity of uniforms and the drugs have fogged your memory, the only thing you remember with any clarity is the way the pain seemed to compress you, to push out and crush in simultaneously, the sudden relief of the head breaching the confines of your pelvis and the body gushing out. She's looking at you now, as you stumble over your words, as your husband stares at anything but her face.

'We don't know yet.'

She made you say it. Out loud.

She lifts the yellow waffled blanket, begins to undo the nappy to peer inside. You watch from the bed, sore, exhausted, at the assumed authority in her fingers. She stitched you back up, she has the upper hand in so many ways here. This is her territory.

'Hmm. Well, there's a thing. Not seen one of those before, in all my days. First time for everything.' She does the nappy back up as if she's packing a sandwich, practical movements with no inherent tenderness. As she tucks the blanket tight around the lump that is your first child you think *please leave, please leave now* but you have to wait for her to pack her bag and say a gentle 'Well, good luck,' before you can blow out the stale breath caught in your chest.

Your husband has taken up the void she left, leaning over, peering. You wriggle and try to get comfy but the bed resists, refuses to contour, and the pad is an uncomfortable wedge between your thighs. You feel sticky and want a shower, some make-up, a drink. Sleep. But the baby is making tiny noises, like an animal snuffling in a hedgerow, and your breasts are leaking yellow stains onto the hospital gown.

The lack of a ready-made personal pronoun halts you. Your mind is blank to the options, but a bleat from the cot forces your mouth to work outside of your brain.

'Pass it here.'

The word *it* hangs in the air in italics, or neon. Mark lifts a hand as if to swat it away, like a troublesome fly, but really he is running his hand through his hair and biting his lip. You both turned away at the twenty-week scan, determined to buck the trend and be surprised, to keep people at work placing bets, to keep parents and aunties and siblings waiting for the news before they could go shopping.

Despite the miasma of tiredness that clouds your vision you are assaulted by a brutal, internal clarity, a revelation of your own, joint pretentiousness. The way you played on your surname, Schroeder. The way you declared, swollen with promise and mystery, that you were a living version of Schrodinger's thought experiment. Explaining to the rapt (or sometimes patient) audience the premise of the classic thought experiment: *Until the birth I am carrying both a boy and a girl! We won't know which until we open the box!*

At the scan the radiologist had reassured you there was no need to keep your eyes closed. 'He or she is hiding it anyway, legs crossed. Little tinker, this one.'

Why didn't you use that name just now? Little Tinker. That's what you've been calling the baby inside you for the last eighteen weeks. Tinker.

Mark scoops the bundle up in his giant hands, his tongue caught between his teeth as if he's performing a delicately technical task. When the weight is fully supported by your billowing stomach he huffs out his own sour breath in relief. You pull up the nightgown and push a nipple into its mouth, concentrating on the technique the midwife showed you, alarmed by the fact the baby is still coated in streaky white vernix. You rub a smudge of blood from its forehead and try to bond. The baby can't focus its eyes yet, closes them against the glare of synthetic light above.

'Did you tell anyone?'

'I called my mum earlier,' there is a hint of panic

somewhere behind the creases of his eyes, 'she's left about ten messages. She knows you were in labour.'

'Tell her false alarm. We're early anyway. We've got a couple of weeks.'

He thumbs his phone to text, hand shaking. You haven't looked yet, not properly. When he's finished texting he turns off the phone.

'So then, what do we call it?' he says. The second time the word is used, it cements the meaning. You've both acknowledged the problem, even though the implications are still lost in the future. None of the names on the shortlist are quite right.

After an hour, during which the baby wakes and cries, and you attempt your first post-natal wee in the tiny en-suite beside the bed, they come to move you. The baby is bound in the yellow blanket until only a marbled pink circle of face is visible, then placed back in the plastic cot. You are told to put your dressing gown on and offered a wheelchair. You check for stains before you ease yourself in, the echo of birth present in the pain from your groin as you sit. The nurse insists on wheeling the cot, and a porter takes you. Mark tries to keep up, side-lined. His job is to carry your bag.

You pass the ward, where it is visiting time. Through the double doors you see two rows of pink and blue balloons, families passing colour-coded parcels of male and female flesh around while mothers and fathers beam. You feel cheated. Not because your baby is different – something primal and angry inside is defensive of its status, fiercely protective – but because no one is here to bring you flowers and tiny little onesies, to argue over whose eyes your child has inherited. *George Bush*, you think, as they steer you into a private room and close the door. *Or Georgina.*

'There we go, love,' the nurse says. 'A bit of privacy for you.'

The room is bare. No, there are pictures on the wall, a TV and an easy chair, monitors and machines sitting mute in the corner, leads looped and trailing. But there are no foil balloons or flowers, no teddies still with their tags on. The nurse pushes the cot up close to the bed and looks around at you and Mark, unsure what you have done to earn this unplanned and unpaid-for privilege. The room is a late assigning. She checks the notes, glancing at the cot before reading them again. 'Dinner will be around in about an hour. Do you want me to see if they can do something for you too?' Mark nods. The porter has gone, and she leaves too.

You pull the blanket over your deflated belly and reach for the remote. You are too tired to think. You want your mum, or a version of her anyway: a version that would hug you and tell you it doesn't matter, that all that counts is good health and the right number of fingers and toes. But you know she wouldn't say this. She would demand to see a consultant, insist on a recount. Tell you it's a modern disease, all this gender neutrality, as if it's your fault, as if you decided to gestate a child of indeterminate sex just to spite her. No, the doctor is right, it's best to wait. You're glad she's so far away.

Mark pulls the chair up close to the bed and holds your hand, squeezes it with just the right amount of pressure to bring tears to your eyes. Not of pain, but because the tenderness of his touch fills you with gratitude that he is here, that it is him beside the bed and no other, lesser man. You feel, at least, that it is both of you being punished for your hubris and humour, that you are in this together. You feel, for the first time since your child was parted from you and the medical team gathered to confer and examine the product of your womb, that if the joke is on you it is at least a collective you, and this brings with it a surge of such love for your husband that you have to bite down hard on your lip to suppress a sob.

You watch the TV together until the smell of mass-produced food overwhelms your senses. Tepid chips and soggy battered fish has never tasted so good. Mark raises a small plastic carton of orange juice and makes a toast.

'To baby Schroeder.'

You follow suit with your own drink, peeling back the plastic seal first so you can both sip after touching the cartons together. You splash the blanket, small yellow stains like bile. The juice is warm and stings your throat. You drink about a pint of water and then regret it, knowing that when you need to wee again it will sting like hell because of the stitches.

The next day they take blood, pricking the baby's heel and squeezing it with blue nitrile-gloved hands until it blooms and beads and is soaked into their test strips. You are waiting to hear when they will discharge you, desperate to get out of the room, but also clinging on to the safety it assures, the anonymity. When they have taken away the samples Mark rocks the baby in the crook of his arm to settle the crying. He gives up after a few minutes, when you say 'Pass it here,' and ease out a swollen breast. You want to feed to relieve the pressure as much as anything.

'We need a name,' he says.

'Is there any point? We need to know first.'

'I hate calling it "it".'

'Me too, but until we know…'

'What about one of those names that is used for both, like Leslie, or Steph?'

You think of your uncle Leslie, of the smell of coffee on his breath as he bent to kiss you, full on the lips, every time he visited. Of the way your mother never left you alone in a room with him.

'Not Leslie. And Steph is too, I don't know… Nineties?'

'Evelyn?'

'That's a girl's name.'

'Nope, I think it's both. Evelyn Waugh was a bloke, wasn't he?'

'Still, we live in Croydon, not Kensington.'

'Alex?'

You look down at the enigma in your arms. The name floats in the air but doesn't settle. You're shaking your head before you even realise it's not the name of your child.

'Blake? Aubrey?'

'Seriously? How much do you want it to get thumped at school?'

Mark laughs, and you join in. The absurdity of the situation overwhelms you both, and you laugh so hard the baby is bounced against you and begins to cry.

'I know how you feel, little one,' you croon through tears, 'I feel it too.' For the first time you feel something like love. Something, but not quite. You had it all worked out, high expectations of the grand reveal. When the narrative turned you had no back-up plan. A part of you is angry that you opened the box (with such epic effort, a seemingly mythological task that should be written into ancient tomes, pored over by academics in dusty libraries, spoken of in keynote speeches) only to find another box.

You move the baby around to switch breasts, feel the latch and the prickle as the milk lets down. There is nothing in the shape of your firstborn to guide you either way – everything is generic: round cheeks and chubby thighs. It could be either. It could be anyone's.

The child sucks with the intensity of all organisms determined to thrive; selfish and unmoved by the discomfort and pain the incessant, rhythmic tug that tongue and palate exert on your nipple, like knives through your chest. You are tired from laughing, from the night before during which you barely slept for the sounds coming from the plastic container beside you, and the sound of the other babies on the ward beyond. When the tiny mouth releases your nipple with a soft wet pop, the head lolling back in a milk-drunk stupor, you gesture to Mark to take over, curl up on your side with your back to the cot and try to sleep. Sleep when the baby sleeps, that's what the websites say.

A knock wakes you. There is a stranger at the door and Mark is nowhere to be seen. The woman walks in without invitation, heads straight for the cot and croons.

'Ah, what a sweetie! Boy or girl?'

You answer without thinking, half asleep, dazed enough for the memory of your wish for a girl to inform your response.

'Oh, she's so pretty! Here,' and the woman, whose hair is so carefully styled and sprayed in place it could be a hat, reaches down into the wheeled trolley she has dragged into the room and pulls out a pink blanket. She drapes it over the baby-shaped body in the crib and picks up a polaroid camera. You are still rubbing your eyes as she shakes out the print.

'Now, here's baby's first photo. And a welcome pack for Mummy. Just fill out the forms inside and post them off, and you'll be a member. Lots of discounts for you. What's her name?'

'We haven't decided yet.'

'Oh well, plenty of time. What an angel, such a good girl letting you sleep.'

She puts the pack on the bed, on your feet. It's heavy, but you can't shift yourself in case it slides off. She holds out the picture and smiles through glossy lips. 'Congratulations!' and she's on her way out. You reach for the nearest missile, throw a cellophane-wrapped pack of paper knickers as hard as you can at the closing door. You look at the photo and realise, it is the first one. Twenty-nine hours after the birth and this is the first one, a hasty snap of a girl you don't recognise. This is either the first image of your daughter, or a picture of your son in drag. The foetal scans don't count. This is your first sin of motherhood, the first step in messing up your child. Guilt spurs love. You shove the picture under your pillow and reach to remove the pink blanket. It's cheap fabric, mass produced. You shove it under your pillow too, to protect Mark. To save you both the conversation.

Other mums are being discharged. You watch through the window of your private room as they strap pink or blue snowsuits into expensive car seats, as dishevelled dads carry the new, fragile loads cautiously, the first time they are allowed to carry them at all.

Doctors come and go, sometimes barely taking the time to introduce themselves or say hello before unwrapping the baby and discussing, heads together, what they are going to do to fix the problem you have made. Twice they wheel the cot away, telling you they just need to consult, and you sit, anxious, wondering what they will bring back. Mark keeps disappearing to call people, to make excuses to the family and friends about why they can't come over. You have flu, he tells them. *Best to stay away. We'll let you know when there is any news.* He goes home once a day to collect the mail and feed the cat. The neutered cat.

You sit on the bed in your fleece pyjamas and massage lotion into your freshly bathed baby. Everything smells right, but you might as well be basting a chicken. The flesh is supple and plump, the legs drawn up, exposing the area that should inform the name. You can't make out any definition, although if you had to decide yourself, you'd say it was probably a boy, or would be a boy. There are folds of flesh, prominent, above what might be labia. You don't explore further. It looks unfinished, half-baked. You wonder, if the birth had not been two weeks early, whether the extra time inside could have unravelled the mystery. You cover the area with a nappy and gently force waving fists through tiny, white sleeves.

'In Sweden they have a third option, instead of *he* or *she*.' Mark has been googling, running down the battery on his phone. 'They use "hen" as a gender-neutral pronoun. We could do that until we know, until the tests come back?'

'Hen? Don't you think that *is* a gendered word in English, though?'

You try not to think of Sunday roasts.

'It's "they" in the non-binary community…' his voice trails off, both of them thinking that the word isn't adequate, implies plural. A child deserves a pronoun of its own.

Mark turns back to his phone, seeking answers. You examine the curve of the baby's eyelashes. They are dark and long, but not especially so. The doctors have told you they will operate soon, to assign a gender. They are waiting on the genetic test results, but say it doesn't really make a difference – they will have to get a specialist to assess the options and do their best with the 'physical material' available. Whether they can better shape a penis or a vulva out of the ambiguous mound inside the nappy will determine what colour icing will adorn future birthday cakes, the statistical chances of success at college, career prospects, suicide risk. No one has mentioned the possibility of grandchildren.

'It's quite fashionable these days to have a gender-neutral name. Think about it: Apple, River, Leaf. What about something like that? Here's one. Sage.'

'Sage?' You try not to think about stuffing, about hens and olive oil and other condiments. The baby looks at you and seems to focus for the first time, the George Bush squint replaced by two blue-black circles that settle on your gaze and hold it. Something leaps inside you, a flip, like the first flutter of movement nine weeks in.

'Hello,' you say, 'hello there.'

You prop it up against your raised knees and look at one another. A drool of milky spit oozes from the corner of its mouth. You reach for a muslin cloth and wipe it away. Everything is yellow, beige, or white. Everything is pure, for now.

'What did you really want?' you ask your husband. 'A boy or a girl?'

'If we could've chosen, you mean?'

'Yes. Which one?'

'I was hoping for a boy. But now? Now I just don't want them to cock it up and pick the wrong one.'

You look at him and he has aged ten years in the last two days. You realise that he has spent more time considering the situation than you, that his phone has opened up a whole world of potential trouble down the line. While you have been negotiating the changes to your body, the physical needs of the baby, he has been considering the long-term impact on its life.

'I don't understand why they choose the gender based on the ease of the operation. Surely it's genetic. X and Y or X and X. Or even deeper, in its soul. It's inside, right?' you ask him.

Mark glances up from his phone. 'I think it's more complicated than that. It might be XY but testosterone levels, or uptake, or something means it will still be more feminine.

So making it a boy might mean it feels wrong, emotionally, when it hits puberty. Or the other way around.'

You haven't considered puberty. You shouldn't have to consider this for years. It's not part of the deal, you think, to worry about surging hormones while the clip is still attached to the slowly shrivelling scrap of umbilical cord. The baby's weight becomes unbearable and you pass it over to Mark, who is getting more confident, comfortable, holding his child. You wish it was still inside, that you still had another week of heaving your bulk up from the sofa to wee every half an hour, and eating Quavers (hell, how many packets of Quavers have you eaten in the last few months?) without feeling guilty, with relish even. Indulging in the sensuality of pregnancy, the aches and glorious rotundity all promising a grand unveiling, a party of sorts.

'So, what if they pick wrong?' you say. 'What if we spend the next ten or so years buying party frocks and bloody Tiny Tears dolls and then our daughter turns around one day and asks why we let a doctor chop her willy off? What if our son gets bullied for hating football? For stealing my make-up?'

Mark is lost in the baby's spell, his face relaxed into a beatific smile. You realise you've become shrill, panicky. That you are on a countdown to being told both your baby's sex and the repercussions. Any minute a doctor could walk through the door and tell you that you are going to have a girl or boy.

'What if we don't do it?' Mark's voice is quiet, lilting. Baby speak. He isn't looking at you, it's as if he's asking the baby.

'What?'

'What if we tell them we want to wait?'

'Can we do that?'

'It's our baby. What's the rush?'

'But, I thought they were going to operate. Soon, like this week.'

'They don't need to. It can pee, and poop. It's feeding well.'

'But they said...'

'They've said lots of things, but they've never asked, have they? They've never given us the third option.'

'Which is?'

'We wait, we see what happens. Whether it becomes a he or she, or chooses to be neither. Or both.'

'And in the meantime?'

'We pick a name and get on with it.'

It all sounds so simple, you could kick yourself for not coming up with the idea yourself. You feel a rush of excitement, the promise of home, of celebrating the fact that you've had a healthy, bouncy baby, that you are a family. Nothing else matters.

'And what do we tell people?'

'The truth? They either accept it, or they can fuck off. Yes, they can fuck off, can't they?' The last sentence is addressed to the baby, with a smile and a gentle bounce.

When the nurse comes in to bring the menu for the evening meal you are the one who says, 'We want to check out now. We're leaving. We won't be here for dinner.'

You pack together, as if packing for a holiday, a tingle of excitement because you don't know where you're going. The doctors come, three of them, to discuss your decision. Two are strongly against, one looks pleased. Progressive, she says, you're right not to rush. Let the baby decide when it's ready, let it be whatever is right in time. She is the only one to smile at the baby, to take a moment to see its face. The validation gives you both the lift you need.

Mark dresses the baby in a yellow snowsuit. As he clips the straps on the car seat together, you speak.

'Sunny.'

'Huh?' His tongue is between his teeth, concentration furrowing his brow.

'We could call it Sunny. Or is that too hippy-ish?'

'I was thinking Kit. Could be short for Christopher or Katherine.'

'Kit Shroeder.'

'Sounds good, don't you reckon? Successful. I can see it on a name plate, or the spine of a book.'

You roll the name around your mouth and mind, peer into the eyes that fix on you as soon as you are within range.

'I like it. I actually like it.'

Mark disappears into the en-suite and although the door is closed you can hear the steady gush of urine hitting the water in the pan. You lean into the cot and inhale the scent of the baby's head.

'Hello, Kit.'

Something clicks. Your breasts leak in response, a prickle and then the spread of warmth into the cotton pads inside your bra. When Mark comes out of the en-suite, still drying his hands on a blue paper towel, you are crying and smiling at the same time. He strokes your shoulder.

You walk past the ward and ignore the noise and colours. Tonight will be for you and Mark, a takeaway and your own sofa, the first night together with Kit in a wooden crib beside your nice wide bed. Tomorrow you will announce the birth and welcome visitors. You'll tell them, as the years roll on, to just buy toys. Not pink plastic kettles and irons, or blue and grey toolkits with chunky, soft ended screws, but anything. Anything that's on offer.

You shiver when you step outside. The carefully controlled temperature of the hospital, of the maternity unit, is sealed away behind the sliding glass doors. It's cold, and curled leaves swirl in circles. A taxi is ticking over in the pick-up bay. Mark carries the car seat and you shoulder the bag. He leans in, checks the seatbelt three times and adjusts the handle to act as a roll cage, just in case. You both sit in the back, holding hands over the sleeping child between you.

'Where to, mate?'

You give the address, even though he's looking through the rear-view mirror at your husband.

You've barely left the hospital grounds when the taxi driver speaks again.

'So, love. Boy or girl?'

A SUDDEN RUSH OF AIR

'What the hell are those?'

Kate spoke before she'd even taken off her coat; she'd just dumped her bag on the desk and walked straight to the window, the same routine she followed every day. She stood with one hand on her top button staring at the wide stone sill, the place she usually scattered lunch crumbs and biscuits for the pigeons.

'Building preservation. The bird shit was eroding the stone.' Across their facing desks Mike was already half a coffee down and had pastry flakes hanging like confetti in his beard. Kate looked at him and huffed a sigh, before pushing up the heavy sash window and reaching out a finger to touch one of the long, grey steel spikes that now sprouted like a vicious, fungal growth along the length of the sill. Hundreds of them, regular and military. The edges of each clipped tip sharp. She sucked her finger where a tiny drop of blood was blooming and slammed the window down hard, noting with a wince the sudden flurry of wings on the street below in response to the sound.

'Bloody hell. I go away for a few days and come back to what? When did they do this?'

'All the buildings are getting them. Keeps the pests away. They came on Thursday.' Mike folded the last half of his croissant and shoved it into his mouth. 'How was the course?'

Kate watched him carefully brush the crumbs off his shirt and tie, out of his neat beard and into the bin, and then clean his hands with a wet-wipe. He gave the desk a quick wipe over and began typing.

'Fine,' she replied, 'the usual: accept there's an issue, stay calm, smile and listen, prepare to compromise. The same as last year.'

She stood and looked out into a cool blue sky and felt empty. The windowsill was silent, the usual cooing and flapping nothing more than a distant echo. She turned away to the coat hook and fussed with her buttons, trying to clear a sudden surge of tears with rapid blinking. In her coat pocket there was a folded sheet of kitchen roll protecting a few crusts of toast stuck together with a smudge of butter. The remnants of Steve's breakfast. If she hadn't scooped them up to feed the birds they'd still be lying on the plate by the sink when she got home.

She flicked the switch on the kettle and tried to smile when Mike held out his cup and said, 'If you're brewing…', letting the roar of boiling water drown out the running commentary on his inbox while her own PC loaded. When she finally sat at her desk opposite him, she turned automatically for a glimpse of the pigeons. She'd worked at the housing association for long enough to recognise some of them, the regulars. There was White-throat and Chequers, Snow-bird and Hopper. Somewhere near the pavement below she thought she saw a swirl of wings, but it could have been litter. When she opened up her inbox there were three messages from home already.

The builders have cancelled for next week. Going to be another month now. Twats.

Where are my trainers? Need to go to the gym later...

Get milk on your way home later, we've run out.

She sighed again and answered them all in one reply. *Bollocks. No idea. OK.* She didn't add a kiss, they'd stopped doing that months ago. When she looked up from her screen Mike was staring at her.

'Cheer up, it might never happen.'

'What makes you think I'm not cheerful?'

'You keep sighing.'

'Sighing is good for you, Mike. In fact, you'd die if you didn't sigh.'

'Right.' He stretched the word, his raised eyebrows telling her she was at it again. He paused, patiently, and let her continue.

'Seriously. It's a reflex in the lungs, like a pacemaker. Everyone does it, about twelve times an hour. Without a variety of breathing rhythms, we'd die.'

'Fascinating. Did you hear that, Viv? Kate reckons her sighing is all that's keeping her alive.' His eyes flicked back to the computer screen.

Viv dropped her large handbag onto her own desk with a thud and sighed herself. She had a sheen of sweat breaking through her make-up and as usual began the day with an apology.

'Sorry. Tram was late. And Tony's never bloody ready on time.'

'Do you want a cuppa?' Kate asked, as eager as Mike to end the conversation. She turned away from them both, busying herself with teabags and sugar to avoid the risk of Viv catching her eye, seeing the something behind the sigh, something she'd been trying to hide for the last few months, and asking her about it.

'Yes please, love. Three sugars.'

'I thought it was two?'

'That was yesterday. I need three today. I've had a bloody awful night with my hip...'

The kettle drowned out the rest of the story.

At lunchtime Kate waited for Mike to go to the staff toilet, then slipped out. She thought she heard Viv call out as the door swung shut, but tightened her jaw and kept going.

As she walked through reception she heard a woman complaining about the wait, her baby griping in the buggy beside her. There was a holdall and three carrier bags overflowing with clothes and toys on the row of stained bench seats behind her. She heard the receptionist sigh, telling her in a practised tone to please sit, they'd be with her as soon as they could.

The woman turned back to her child and muttered, loud enough for the whole room to hear, an obscenity Kate hadn't heard for weeks. The kind of word you say when you have nothing left to lose.

'Madam, if you continue to behave in an aggressive manner, we will have you escorted from the premises.'

Kate scurried past, through the fog of desperation and frustration that drifted around the woman and child like cigarette smoke, and into the busy market street beyond. The charity shops and cafés were obscured by the stalls, striped awnings and tables overflowing with homewares. Clothes on steel racks twisted and turned in the wind.

She shivered and pulled her coat tighter, glancing around for somewhere to sit. Pigeons strutted and limped between the shoppers, and she looked up to see three circling near the window of her office. She watched them until someone bumped into her and called her a bitch.

There were three people already sitting on the nearest bench, each separated by curved metal arm rests. She stood nearby waiting for someone to get up and leave, shifting her weight from foot to foot, then reached into her pocket for the crusts and tipped them on to the cobblestones at her feet. Immediately the birds gathered, some eager to eat and others with puffed out chests, purring and courting the females. Last year she'd heard the scratch and scuttle of claws on the sloping roof above the staff toilet, found that if she leaned out of the window she could see a nest. She'd checked every day after that, watched the tiny, monstrous chicks fluff up and then smooth over into this year's adults.

As they surged around her feet she thought about home, about the changes that had been made, were being made, the many little jobs he'd started since he moved in, abandoned half-finished. Peeling wallpaper and broken tiles. 'It'll add value to the house,' he'd say, but so far all she felt was a slow erosion. Sharp edges and new textures that left her unable to settle in the evening. More things to clean up, to put away, and his petulant response when she left cheery lists pinned to the fridge or circled the classifieds in the local paper. Rubbish removal, plasterers, decorators. 'Don't waste money on that,' he'd say. 'I'll do it.' But he never did. She thought about calling the builders when she went back up, about buying something special for dinner on her way home. She thought about anything other than the wary negotiations of his mood and the effort she put into trying to make him happy, the amount of times she failed. Once the builders started on the extension it might get better, spur him to action. He might enjoy the company, become brisk and make tea, clean up for when she got home.

She was just about to go back inside and eat her lunch at the desk like she did every day, when a small boy ran straight in front of her, arms out and screeching with delight at the panic he caused. The pigeons flapped and rose in a clumsy cloud of fear, circling away, finding nowhere safe to rest. Kate looked around at all the windowsills along the street, saw each one glinting with the same barbs. Wrapped her arms tight around herself and stalked back to the microwave-meal miasma of the office, to Mike's latest opinions on the migrant crisis and Viv's *Daily Mail* agreement that yes, it's all someone else's fault.

Back home, she sat in the driveway for almost three minutes before she could muster the energy to get out of the car and face whatever state the house was in.

Less than a year ago her home had been quiet, ordered. The

garden fell away to fields and a small pond for the toads and frogs in spring was surrounded by wildflowers. She hadn't done much to the house in her years there, just kept it simple and tidy, with plenty of pot plants. When Steve had moved in conversation and wine replaced chores, and his hands pulled her away, into lazy evenings on the sofa or early nights. *Leave it, I'll do it later* a regular refrain. And she'd been happy to accommodate him, to give him what he needed. Attention, space. Washing the dishes in the morning before she left for work instead. Brought back little treats from the corner shop to lighten his mood after a difficult day. When she tactfully mentioned the slow build of stale cigarette smoke that seeped into the curtains and sofa, that she smelled in her own hair, on her own clothes, in the office, he turned wide brown eyes on her and said, 'I need it babe, I need one vice. It helps me unwind.'

When he said he wanted to work from home she moved her things out of the way, agreed to eat dinner on the sofa every evening, plates balanced on laps, so he could turn her dining table into a desk to Skype call his clients. Files and paperwork where the potted herbs and placemats once sat. He was an online counsellor. Needed quiet to let his patients spill their troubles into her lounge undisturbed. He needed her to support him. At the end of each day he would close the laptop and lean back in the chair while she cleared the coffee cups and plates from around him. She gave him time to unwind, to brood and process the misery he had absorbed while she cooked dinner for them both, or went out again to shop. By early evening he would be smiling again, asking her about her day, although she had begun to be careful what she said for fear of his face falling into a frown.

The curtains were closed.

Kate stepped over his gym bag and flicked on the kitchen light. Flies circled the bare bulb. He hadn't done the dishes or emptied the bin, despite promising her twice he would. She went to the sink before she'd even taken her coat off and turned the tap, filling the bowl with hot water and detergent and sliding plates and cups into the water until their contours breached the bubbles at the surface. She took a damp cloth and wiped crumbs off the counter, all the time listening for a sound that might tell her where he was in the house, what mood he was in.

There was a pile of notepaper beside the laptop on the kitchen table, more cups and a half-eaten sandwich. She took the curling bread and opened the back door, stood in the garden and surveyed the piles of broken tiles and furniture that he'd left there since first starting the improvements, the plan to extend and add a proper office. Kate reached into the tallest shrub and spiked the half sandwich into one of the branches, hoping the birds would see it and flock to eat. When she turned around to go back into the house he was standing in the doorway, holding a dead mouse by the tail.

'Got the little bastard!'

'How?'

'Reset the traps, then used chocolate instead of cheese. One down...' He tossed the limp body into the corner of the garden, where a pile of grass clippings and old shrub cuttings were rotting into slime.

Kate followed him into the house, angry at herself for not tripping the catches on the traps while he slept in late, as she'd done every day since he'd started his vendetta against the mice. He was already wrist deep in the fridge, rummaging for snacks.

'You need to wash your hands.'

He put back a yoghurt pot and sloped over to the sink, dipping his fingers in the steaming dishwater before drying them on the tea towel. She pulled out a dining chair and removed a stack of mail shots before slumping down and releasing the breath she'd been holding in a slow exhalation. When she looked up, he was leaning back on the counter eating yoghurt with a fork.

'What's up with you?'

'Nothing,' she replied, letting her eyes drift over the notes on the table. The laptop hummed.

'You're doing it again.'

'Doing what?'

'Sighing. Like it's the end of the fucking world or something.'

'I need to sigh, everyone needs to sigh.'

'No, it's just you. It's your reaction to everything I do now.'

'Steve, sighing is a natural function. If we didn't sigh, we'd die.'

'Bullshit. Sighing is sarcasm without the effort of words. It's showing you're pissed off without having to say why.'

'There's a pacemaker inside us, Steve. It triggers about once every five minutes or so. It varies our breathing so we get the right amount of oxygen, so that our alveoli don't collapse.'

'And there you go again. Alveoli. There's always a fact with you, isn't there? A practicality to fill the void.' He put the yoghurt down behind him and the weight of the fork tipped it over.

Kate watched as the cool creamy liquid oozed out onto the worktop. Felt something inside her tipping too. Finally, she summoned up the strength to speak. 'So, you want to talk now? You're ready? Because every time I've asked you what's wrong recently you've just said "nothing", said you're "fine".'

For the first time in months he held her gaze without looking away.

'So talk to me. Tell me how work is going? Where are you at with the bathroom you insisted we renovate? Let's talk, Steve.'

He flinched at every word and dropped his head. She felt like that child who had run at the pigeons, suddenly understanding the urge to disrupt the stasis, felt shame at how satisfying it was to speak sharply after months of whispering and holding her tongue. For a moment she almost reached out and apologised for causing him any hurt. But as she looked at him still wearing the clothes he'd slept in the night before her heart rate increased. She felt the throb in her fingertip from the spike on her office windowsill and held in the sigh she was so desperate to release. Instead, she looked beyond him at a spindly spider that hung in the corner of the room, watching it vibrate in its web while she counted slowly in her head and forced her body to relax.

When he looked at her she moved her gaze away quickly, knowing that if he saw the spider he'd swat it with a newspaper, suck it up with the hoover pipe. So she focussed on the floor and waited for him to stop sniffing, ran through her training once more: *stay calm, smile and listen, prepare to compromise*, then asked gently, 'Tell me what's going on. It feels like you're not really here anymore, like this is just a place to sleep and eat.'

In the silence that followed, Kate heard a shout from the

street, the fridge click and hum into life, something creak above her – maybe the wood of a floorboard expanding or contracting a fraction of a millimetre. She could feel something building, a moment about to happen that would change everything, strip her of any control. She sucked in a slow intake of air and spoke.

'Is there someone else?'

He nodded. She felt the wound through her chest, a sharp spike piercing her breast and lodging deep, until she could barely breathe. She held as still as possible, knowing if she moved now she'd explode or crumble. *Calm, smile, listen...* like a mantra. She could only manage two of the three.

'Tell me about her.'

'I don't know what to say.'

'Tell me everything. Tell me from the start. Her name.'

'You know I can't, it's confidential.'

'Confidential?'

'She's one of my patients. Was one of my patients.'

'What happened?'

'I've lost my job.' He gulped and she could tell he had tears in his eyes without looking at them. 'She killed herself three months ago. She left a note...'

Kate concentrated hard on the tiles of the kitchen floor, the steady blue and cream checks, the lines that ran between them. She calculated in their symmetry and form the last few months, the slow slide from some shared goal, some notion of future into awkward silences and moods she couldn't read. Eventually there were evenings when he would ask her not to speak at all, beg her to be quiet. He'd play loud music until she had to ask him to turn it down before her neighbours complained. She'd thought he was depressed. Picked up his shoes and tiptoed past his slumped form on the bed, past the heap of duvet that protected him from conversation. The few times they'd had sex he kept his eyes closed tight, stopped checking her reaction to the increase in rhythm, until his climax was fierce enough to bring him to tears. She'd watch him roll away and turn his back on her and she'd seal her own pain away to deal with later, once he was better. She'd lie in the dark trying to work out how to help him.

'What did it say?'

'She talked about me. Enough to get me sacked. There's an inquest...'

'How did this even happen, Steve? I thought we had...'

'She reminded me of you. That's how it started. She was nineteen and had these cuts all along her arms.'

'I was twenty-seven when we met. I never had cuts.'

'Not externally. But I always thought that beneath it all you were hurting in some way.'

A woodlouse meandered across Kate's field of vision. It blurred as he continued.

'And there was something similar in her eyes, like behind the iris. And she was so wounded.'

'You wanted to save her?'

'It's what I do. I try and save people.'

'But you kill mice?' She heard the venom in her words, and it felt good.

'Mice are not people, Kate. They're vermin.'

She let out a breath, closed her eyes for second and let him continue, determined not to cry, not to rush at him and hit him around his head until he fell silent.

'I guess I let her get under my skin. I let it go too far.'
'How far?'
'Far enough.'
'Did you sleep with her?'
'No. God no. I've never even been in the same room as her. But we developed a... a relationship.'
'When did it start? This relationship. When did it become a relationship?'
'Only a month or so before she, you know...'
'Really?'
'No. Obviously something started before that. I knew she was transferring.'
'And who said it first?' Kate felt the barbs rising to protect her as she waited for an answer, imagined herself armoured with them, like a hedgehog.
'She did. And I told her clearly that it was inappropriate. I told her it was transference.'
'But you didn't report it. You didn't pass her on to a colleague?'
'No. I couldn't let her go. She needed me, and I needed her.'
'Why? You had me!'
'And your facts. Fucking *alveoli*! Christ Kate, I needed to hear someone tell me why they were sad, not just to give a medical explanation of the lungs.'
But even hedgehogs have soft bellies, and her chest felt punctured again. Her breathing shallow, throat tight.
'Are you blaming me? Are you telling me it's my fault you fell for this... this *teenager*?'
'No. Maybe. I always hoped you'd confide in me, let me in. I used to think you needed me.'

'What makes you think I don't? I might not have scars on my arms, but I still need someone to talk to, about work and—'

'Work! Nothing more, nothing deep or... interesting.'

'And so I stopped, because you said you heard enough of it in your job. What should I have done?'

'I don't know, I'm sorry. I never meant to hurt you, or to ruin what we have. What we had.'

'What did you think was going to happen?'

'Nothing. I had no intention to leave you. It wasn't like I was planning to elope or something. She was damaged, and she needed me, she needed someone to love her. So I did.'

'That wasn't what I meant. I meant what did you think would happen to us.'

'I didn't think. I tried not to. I felt like shit if I thought about it, if I thought about you.'

'So you decided not to think about me?'

'Something like that, yeah.'

Kate stood up and began to wash the dishes, tried to lose herself in the cathartic pleasure of seeing the dirt slide off the ceramic patterns of gold circles and twisting ivy beneath the sponge, the bubbles slip down the clean plates as they stood in order on the drainer. She looked out of the window to see if the birds had found the half-eaten sandwich, but it was getting dark, and she could only just make out in silhouette that it drooped, untouched, from the spear of wood. Eventually she couldn't bear his silence anymore.

'What did you talk about?'

'Stuff.'

'What stuff? Not what did she talk about, but what did you say?'

'At first? Not much. She was the one who needed to speak. I just listened and... and absorbed.'

'But there must have been an interchange, a dialogue. You had to give something back.'

'Eventually. But it went beyond words. We'd sit, sometimes for a whole session, just looking at each other through the screen. Or not looking at each other. In silence.'

'And that was enough?'

'Yes and no. The silence gets too loud sometimes. Deafening.'

Kate could see him mirrored in the small window over the sink, the dusk outside a bruised backdrop to his reflection. She pulled the plug and let the choking sound of the water draining away fill the void their voices left in the room.

Holding the damp tea towel like a life ring she asked, 'So why did she...?'

'Because I told her it had to stop. Because I couldn't talk to you anymore.'

Kate sighed without even realising, felt the double intake of breath, one inhalation followed by the lifesaving second gasp that re-inflated her alveoli and kept her alive.

'But I miss her. I love her. Not like I love you, but I do love her. And it's my fault she's gone.'

Kate heard his first sob breach the confines of his throat, but found herself walking away from him, forcing heavy feet to take her upstairs, over the carpet they planned to replace once the builders had been, into the bathroom where side by side they'd stood and hacked the tiles off the walls because he didn't like the colour. Trying to make something new, trying to build something together.

She locked the door and sank to the ground. She could smell his piss in the carpet, and there were tiny shards of ceramic around the edge of the room. Holes in the wall gaped dark and ragged where the plaster had come away with the tile adhesive. There was a pair of his dirty underpants on the floor, where he'd cast them off for a shower. The pain in her chest swelled until she felt like she would choke, or vomit. She couldn't cry, ground her teeth instead and listened to the mice scurry behind the walls, scratching for food, for a cable to chew or some insulation they could shred to line their nests. They'd be breeding soon, maybe already had a litter or two stashed in the attic. She'd waited months to hear him confess, and wished he'd stayed silent.

She peeled a strip of wallpaper from the wall beside her, rolled it between her finger and thumb and imagined the bathroom finished. Pale cream tiles on the floor, soft white on the walls. A new bath to soak in after a sticky day in the office. It wasn't that he'd fallen in love with someone else that hurt. It was the words *she reminded me of you.*

He didn't know her at all if he thought that.

She waited until she heard the front door slam and went down. Cleaned up the yoghurt from the counter and tidied up the table. The notes were all about the inquest. Answers to questions that might be asked. A list of excuses on small yellow post-its. She screwed them up and dropped them in the bin.

Mike was eating cereal at his desk when she entered the office the next morning. He looked up, a few drops of milk caught in his beard. He reached for a paper napkin and wiped his mouth.

'You okay?'

She ignored him and dropped her handbag on the desk, walked straight to the window.

The metal spikes branched out from the sill towards the weak morning sunlight. To the left of centre a pigeon struggled, impaled through the chest. Its wings were ragged from trying to fly away, from beating against the spears either side. It turned and twisted its head, beak wide and blood-foamed.

'Shit! Mike, help me here.' Kate eased the window open and the bird doubled its efforts to escape, claws gripping and pushing at the steel rods. She reached a hand forward to stroke its head, to calm it, but it twisted away as much as it could with three metal barbs embedded in the soft, plump bow of its breast. A gurgle of air escaped its beak. It sagged, exhausted.

'Oh, Jesus. That is vile.' Mike's cornflake breath and aftershave consumed Kate's senses. He was pressed lightly against her, looking over her shoulder to watch the bird's final moments.

'Help me then, we've got to save it.'

'How? I'm not touching it.' She felt his weight shift as he moved away.

'We need to get it off, get it to a vet or something.'

'Vets don't treat pigeons, Kate. Sky rats. It's not like a puppy or something.' She heard him put the kettle on as the bird tried once more to free itself.

'It's still alive! Call someone, or get me a towel or something. If I can just ease it off maybe I can...'

'No, don't do that.' Viv was breathless, sweating. Kate hadn't heard her come in. 'You'll kill it if you do that. The spikes are plugging the wounds. Take it off and it'll bleed out. Poor sod.'

'So what do I do?'

'You'd have to cut the metal, take it in and let the surgeon remove the spikes.'

'How do you know all this, Viv?' said Mike. He scooped out his teabag and dropped it with a wet thud into the metal bin.

'Saw it on *Bizarre ER*. There was this guy who'd fallen on some fencing, right? Well, they said if they lifted him off, he'd bleed to death really quickly. It went in through his thigh and out of the top of his left bum cheek.'

'So how did they do it?' asked Kate.

'Got the fire brigade, sedated him and sawed the fencing. He went in face down on the stretcher, the spike still sticking through him. A human kebab.'

'I'm not calling the fire brigade for a bloody pigeon, Kate. Don't even think it,' Mike warned.

'Well, do you have any bolt cutters? A toolbox or something? There must be something.'

'Do I look like the kind of man to carry bolt cutters? I work for a housing association, not a garage.'

'You'll have to kill it,' Viv wheezed.

'She's right, Kate.'

'Put the poor sod out of its misery,' Viv added.

'I can't.' Kate was shaking, her eyes flitting between the drooping bird and her colleagues as they watched her.

'Well I'm not doing it.' Mike sipped his tea, walked behind his desk and raised his eyebrows.

'There must be some other way, I'm sure if we call a charity or a vet or someone they'll help.'

'They won't, love, not for a pigeon. I hit one once with my car and it was still alive. They told me the kindest thing to do would be to either drive over it again, or carry on and forget about it. They're not bothered about pests.' Viv dropped into her office chair and began to root through her bag.

'Can you...?'

'Oooh, not me. No. I can barely pop a zit without fainting.'

'Wring its neck. One quick twist and it's over with.'

'Mike, I can't...'

'You'll have to. It's your responsibility.'

'How is it?'

'You were the one feeding them every day. It wouldn't be there if you didn't encourage it with your crumbs.'

'But...'

'Face it, Kate, you attract vermin.'

'I didn't know they were going to put spikes on the bloody window though, did I?'

Mike sat down at his desk and started typing. Viv was already sorting through the mail. Through the open window Kate could hear the market vendors calling out in the street below, traffic slowing for the lights, the sudden rush of air being displaced by a dozen or more wings as a flock of pigeons took flight. She reached out and held the bird in her hands as best she could around the spikes. She thought it might be Chequers, but it was hard to tell when the feathers were so ruffled, so damp and torn. She felt it struggle between her fingers, a final attempt at freedom before it gave up. She slid her hands to its neck and twisted. Inhaled once, twice, and let out a long, slow, lifesaving breath.

ANOTHER PLACE

You're sitting in your garden when you see her. She's walking through the dunes that lie beyond the tangled slope of the lawn, and as you twist the stem of a daisy with one hand and twirl your pencil with the other you're distracted by the loose swing of her legs, the way she sweeps her arm around her head to catch her hair and keep it off her eyes.

You drop your head and try to focus on the pages of algebra balanced on your bare knees, but even as your own hair falls around your face you glance up again; you don't really care what the value of x is anyway, and no matter how many times your mam tries to explain, it's clear the purpose of learning algebra is to pass exams, nothing more. You search the space where she was, but she must have gone over the dunes; all you see is the seagrass waving in the breeze, or, you imagine, moving back into place after her hands have trailed through the fine stems and then let go.

Cai is sitting beside you, focussed, small. He moves his lips when he works, and rocks slightly, back and forth. Only slightly. It's as if he is sitting on a raft on an almost still lake, while the rest of you are on solid ground. You are sure this is why you left your last school. Why you are now working on algebra in the garden of another new house during the summer holidays, while every other teenage girl is enjoying the freedom of six weeks without numbers or grammar to cloud their minds.

Being educated at home means no term dates, no timetable. The lines between learning and living are already blurred.

You scribble a final guess at the answer and rub at the bright embroidery neatly hemming your cut-off shorts. This is another reason why you left. The colourful threads holding your clothes together, the time Mam takes to make each item last until you can't do the buttons up anymore, is enough to set you apart and make you a target. The girl on the sand was wearing cut-off shorts too, but hers were frayed at the edges; ripped and threadbare. You know this is how they were on the hanger in the shop. No one punches you for wearing clothes with holes in, unless the holes have been repaired.

You get up. The late July sun is already turning the lawn brown, crisping the tips of the grass. Cai doesn't notice you standing to stretch. Mam is hanging clothes out on the line, will be back at her laptop soon. Working from home. Educating you and your brother in between emails. It's mid-afternoon and you've had enough.

'Can I go for a walk?'

Her frown is quicker than her smile these days. 'Where to?'

'Just the beach.'

'Only if you take the dog. And Cai.'

The dog is big and shaggy, too friendly to protect you, but maybe big enough to deter people from approaching.

'Do I have to?'

'He needs a run out.' She frowns at the dog, another thing on the list of things she doesn't have time for. You didn't mean the dog, but don't want to make things harder for her.

'Okay.'

Cai doesn't really want to leave his work, but is always too eager to please to protest. You wish, as you ease his feet into his rubber sandals, that sometimes he'd kick back like a normal kid. He smiles at you every time you look at him. Most of the time you smile back.

'Please be careful.' Your mam is already regretting saying yes, and you know she'd rather come with you, but has to get back to her desk. 'Don't talk to strangers.'

You roll your eyes at this – you're fourteen – you've lived by this rule for years.

'And stay away from any big groups of kids, you know?'

You know. As if there are gangs here, in Crosby, where old people come to walk their cockerpoos and yorkies, and short-distance tourists come to take photos with Gormley's rusting iron men standing alert and tense along the beach.

Cai holds your hand tight as you push open the garden gate with your knee. The dog pulls hard on the lead. It's looped around your hand, and as your bare feet slide on the sandy slope of the dunes you are trapped between your brother's sticky grip and the rope of the lead digging into your wrist. But the sun is turning the sand to glitter, a cascade of cinnamon and sugar that sifts between your toes and tickles, and the sound of the breeze in the long seagrasses distracts you from the dog crouching to defecate, a whisper of something you don't need to understand, or even hear, to be excited by. You kick sand over the mess because you forgot the bags. At least this house is by the sea; a flat beach with a flat horizon beyond, unlike the rugged coves and forested coastline of Wales where you've spent summers before, but still better than those few noisy years in the city, or the months in the Midlands village where everything smelled of cow shit and rain.

You can smell the sea now the heavy scent of the garden flowers is behind you, and you want to run over the crest of the dune to catch sight of the glittering line of water beyond the beach, but Cai is stalling, bending to grin at every shell, and the dog is yanking your arm out of its socket to sniff at every tuft of grass, cocking his leg every few feet to lay claim to this new territory.

'Come on, Cai.' He doesn't catch the swelling frustration in your tone. He's nearly nine. You're pretty sure any other nine-year-old would refuse to hold hands with their sister. You give him a gentle tug and he squeezes your fingers and speeds up. Then you're over and a gust of wind hits you and whips your hair around your face and you haven't a hand free to sweep around your head to catch it.

The beach is busy. The tide is midway out, and the sand shows an almost straight line between wet and almost dry as it recedes. Gormley's statues stand like sentinels across the bay, some half-buried as the wind and water have shifted the sand over the years, some half-submerged by the incoming tide as if part way through a suicide bid, some up near the dunes, fully exposed from head to toe. You still don't know if they are creepy or marvellous. There are little dogs zipping around, yapping at each other, and people in windbreakers despite the sun, carrying knapsacks. A couple nearby are dragging a toddler, cooing to him as he stumbles between them, taking pictures on their phones to capture his first time on the cusp of land and sea.

And there she is. You hold back, watching. She is standing by one of the rusting iron men, taking a picture with her phone. For a second you consider going over, asking her what she thinks of the repeated, corroding bodies staring out to sea. She half squats to take another shot and you watch. She has on those carefully ripped shorts, a yellow cropped vest that shows, in flashes from the sun, a jewelled piercing through her belly button. A small handbag on a thin strap bounces at her hip. She's wearing slim ballet pumps. You shuffle in the sand, barefoot, your legs covered to the knee by faded denim that is patched and embroidered with flowers and stars. A plain T-shirt keeps the sun off your shoulders.

She grins at the phone and stands up straight, then slips it into the bag and pulls out a single cigarette and lighter, turns her back on the breeze and cups her hands over her face. She notices you staring on the first inhale.

'What?'

You don't reply. You don't know what to say. You start fussing with Cai and hope she thinks she was mistaken when she saw you watching her. When you look up, she's walking over. You've been on the sand for less than ten minutes and already you've lost control of the situation, put you both in danger. You glance around to see if she has friends, if they're going to circle you. The dog pulls towards her, wagging. Useless.

'Hello, big fella. Hello.' She fusses him and laughs when he licks at her wrists and tugs you closer to her.

'Sorry, he's still a pup really. Stupid dog.'

'S'fine. I like dogs.' She sucks the cigarette and looks you up and down. 'Holiday?'

You bark out a laugh before you have the chance to realise it isn't polite. Some people might look forward to a week or more every year on this blank beach, its only interesting feature the lonely clones rotting in the salt water. 'No, we just moved here.'

'What school you at?'

'None.'

'Well, what school you goin' to?'

'I'm not.'

'How old are you?' She's looking you up and down. The shapeless tee, the knee-length shorts. Your naked face already spattered with freckles despite the factor-50 your mam slathers over you every morning. Her face is smooth, a heavy beige that finishes in a smudged line below her jaw.

You shuffle, wish your mam would call you now, give you an excuse to walk away before you have to answer. You stare at the gem at her navel, a pink zirconia. 'We don't go to school. Educated at home.'

'Lucky bugger.' She looks impressed, tilts her head. 'How old are you?'

'Fourteen.'

'Same as me.'

She looks older, but then most of them do. She has little flicks of black kohl at the corner of each eye, and although her face is generic, rounded with a soft nose, she has added cheekbones with bronzer, has a sheen of gloss on her lips. Your mam would never let you go out like this. *Dressed like a working girl.*

'I've got to walk the dog.' You know how lame this sounds. Excusing yourself has become a habit. What you really want is to go back to her house and listen to music with swear words, learn how to make your face look a different shape just by adding shadows from a palette, but you know you can't.

'I'll walk with you. Come on.' She looks back at you as she

heads towards the point where the sea and sand meet. When you catch up, she has slipped off the pumps and is staring at another one of the statues, this one with its feet submerged in sand and shallow water.

Cai stoops to dabble fingers in the water, still gripping your hand and pulling your shoulder down as he drops, so you are lopsided. The dog cocks its leg against the metal man. The girl whoops with laughter. 'That's boss, that is. Wish I'd got that on my phone.'

You wish you had a phone. You try and tug Cai away from the water. The sand is crumbling beneath your feet.

'Why don't you let him off?'

You're not sure, at first, if she's talking about Cai or the dog. 'He might run away.'

'Nah, we can get him back.' She unclips the dog's lead without asking and he lopes off, snapping at the little ridges of waves. You feel the sag of the lead in your hand like it's you who has just been cut loose, and it's exhilarating and terrifying. You don't realise you're breathing hard and chewing your lip until you taste blood.

'You need to chill. Here.' She holds out the last stump of her cigarette and you nearly take it, out of politeness, but Cai looks up at you and holds out a small pink shell the shape of an ear, and you use this distraction to avoid the offer. As you crouch down to look at the shell you are right next to her legs, see the subtle streaks in their tone that must be fake tan, the orangey stain around the rough skin of her knees, the soft prickle of new growth hair that looks like fine sand stuck all the way up her shins. You nearly reach out to brush the skin, to see if it actually is sand giving her legs that sugar-dusted texture.

'You wanna be careful, turn your head the wrong way and it'll have your eye out!' She's laughing and you look up to see why. She points back at the statue, at the oxidised metal penis hanging out and down from the crotch of the artist's cast like a spigot, level with your face.

You feel blood rush to your neck and cheeks and stand up, dropping Cai's hand so you can distance yourself from the solid, drooping genitals. The statue has been transformed by its time in the water; there are tiny shells clustered around its thighs, threads of bright green seaweed in the rough surface of its hips. You feel embarrassed for it, a compulsion to cover it up. But that's not the point of the installation. From the project Mam set you before you moved here you know they are all about exposure, and its effects. Only the sea and the sand are allowed to cover them.

'So what's your name then?' She's looking around like she's bored, waiting for something more interesting to focus on.

'Morgan.' You wait for the inevitable.

'That's a boy's name.'

'No, it's Welsh. It means *dweller of the sea*.'

'Dweller of the sea? Like a crab? Or a bloody jellyfish!' She's laughing at you now, not with you. 'You must feel right at home here then.'

How do you explain that nowhere feels like home anymore? You've moved so many times, home is in the bottom of a cardboard box, never quite unpacked.

'What's he called then?'

'Cai.' You don't say his full name. Mordecai. It's not worth the conversation.

'And what does that mean then?' She's squinting at you, lips closed in a smile that might be mocking you, or interested.

'Warrior.'

She snorts. 'Looks like a warrior, don't he?'

The dog is getting further away, his shape becoming indistinct, generically dog-like. Cai is drifting too, now you are no longer tethering him with your hand. He's foraging, stuffing his pockets with shells and pebbles, moving sideways like a crab. You go and stand over him, protective. She follows, slowly, placing each foot carefully like she's walking down a runway in a fashion show. If you lose the dog your mam will never let you out alone again.

'I'm Jess. Nothing special in that.' Her tone has an edge. Defiant. Proud.

'I bet it is. You should look it up.'

She gives you a withering glance and then turns a slow circle in the sand. 'It's shit here, isn't it?'

'It's alright.'

'How long you been here?'

'Two months.'

'Bet it feels like years already. It'll get worse. S'alright when the weather's like this. Give it a bit, then you'll hate it. We all do.'

'Where do you live?' It's the first question you've asked her, and you feel a sudden surge of confidence that you've breached this point, made it a conversation instead of an interrogation.

She waves a hand back towards the dunes, and stares at Cai. 'What's wrong with him then?'

'Nothing's *wrong* with him. He's just... quiet.'

The dog is standing half in and half out of the sea, staring at the horizon. You swing the lead in your hand, the clip weighting the end like a pendulum. The rhythm soothes you. As you move your feet you feel the sand suck at your toes, the water clouding like milky coffee.

She's staring down at Cai, watching him lining up pebbles under the shallow water, his lips moving as he counts and describes each one under his breath. He scuttles away a bit and she follows. You can't move, your feet are sinking, and the wind has picked up and is wrapping your hair around your face so that you can only see things in blinks and flashes: the blueness of the sky, the white light bouncing off the water near the horizon, the flat brown sand. You should call the dog and drag Cai back home, rinse his feet off with the hose and change your clothes, but your whole body feels slow, like it's switched into a different mode. The people walking past seem to be on fast forward. She's bending down to Cai and offering him something.

'He can have sweets, can't he? Not going to go mental 'cos of the additives?'

'Mam doesn't like us to...'

Cai reaches up and takes the bright jellies from her hand, stuffs them into his wide gurning mouth.

She laughs, 'I think he likes them! Kids need a treat every now and then, don't they?'

You stand mute, watching as she takes his hand and begins leading him towards the water. His feet are submerged, then his ankles. He's looking up at her and laughing, and she's smiling back, chatting, pointing things out to him with a perfectly manicured nail. The words are torn up in the breeze, leaving only syllables and consonants floating loose and flapping away.

You glance down at the circle of space around your ankles. There are tiny shards of shell, smashed on rocks in the tide and slowly becoming sand as they fracture against each other, miniscule strands of coloured weed threading out in the last dying reach of the waves, and, as your eyes adjust to the micro-world by your toes, little sand shrimps and water creatures puttering around, appearing and disappearing as they bury themselves and emerge.

As you watch, the waves recede further and further until the only water left is held in the sand, and the tops of your feet are exposed to the air. Goosebumps texture the pale skin. You look up and compare the view, the big wide-open space around you unaware of the tiny world at your feet; people passing each other, pausing to take photographs, yelling at their dogs or kids to come back; the beach's wide accumulation of sand stretching beyond the curve of the bay. And the sky, so vast that if you look for too long you could tip and fall. Those metal monsters, and you, are the only things not moving.

When you look around for Cai, and the dog, you see the three of them together, so far out. Cai's shorts must be wet, he's up to his thighs, and the dog is leaping around her, splashing and barking. She's spinning, her hair swirling out, and you can see the gaping laugh as she loses her balance, staggers, and then finds her feet again. They are small, distant, and you are alone. You try to move but the sand clings to you, and it seems to take a gargantuan effort to release your feet, the suck and glug of the wet sand sending a warning signal: a few moments more and you'd be lost, sucked down. You watch beige sludge fill the footprints, the slow ooze of all those wet grains pooling to erase your presence.

You start walking towards them, try once to call out but find your throat dry, tight. The waves are shallow at first, slow. As you walk you send out waves of your own, the energy moving out of your legs and into the water, dissipating. As you get deeper you can feel the movement of the sea against you, instead of the other way around. It pushes at your shins, your knees, gently but insistently. Telling you to go back. The hems of your shorts are sucking up the sea water, clinging to your thighs and making it hard to walk. But there he is, Cai, up to his waist, reaching up to touch one of the half-buried statues on the exposed, corroded shoulder.

As you struggle through the swell she lets go of his hand and he goes under, his dark head swallowed and lost in the grey surface of the sea. For a second everything goes quiet, and you hold your breath. You feel lightheaded, loose. You look around but she's not looking, is staring at the horizon with a half-smile on her lips. Then you lunge forward, catch his arm just as he bobs back up and gasps. When he sees you he grins, even though you can hear his breathing is fast and gurgling as you wrap your arms around him and lift him up. He clings to you like a monkey. The dog is swimming in wide circles around you.

'What the hell are you doing, bringing him out this far?' It's meant to be a shout, an accusation. Your own breathing is ragged, and tears are threatening to humiliate you.

'He's fine. Look at him smiling. Fuck's sake, what's your problem?'

'It's too deep.'

'Too deep for you, dweller of the sea?'

'He could have drowned!'

She rolls her eyes and flicks water at you. It's freezing cold, and as it spatters across your chest you gasp. Your T-shirt clings to you, exposing the curve of your still-blooming breasts, the nipples hard as pebbles in the wind. You pull the fabric away with one hand while clinging on to your brother with the other.

'He was having fun.'

You can feel him shivering against you. When you look at him he's still smiling, but his lips are changing colour: purple, blue.

'He could have drowned.' It's almost a sob.

'So what?' She comes close, stares you down. 'Then you wouldn't have to…'

'Don't say it. Do not say it.'

'…hold his hand all the time.' She smiles and flicks water at you, turns to walk away. Cai struggles against you to follow her. Twists his little wet fist out of yours and reaches up to her. He slips off your hip, stumbles and splashes. She takes his hand and starts walking inland. Her shorts are soaked, clinging to her backside, and you watch, mesmerised, for a second before running after them.

'Give him back.'

'I'm not taking him away. We're just walking, aren't we kid?' Looking down at him, beaming those glossy lips. He grins up at her.

You struggle to keep up, your long shorts are heavy with saltwater, pulling you down. Seaweed tangles around your feet. You look down at the soupy mess your movement is making in the water, and it disgusts you.

'He's not yours!' you shout, and she stops and glances back.

'S'okay, I don't want him.'

You don't catch up until you reach the hard sand, the point where the wind is drying the surface and blowing it away. Crisp packets and black twists of dried seaweed tumble past. She's crouching opposite Cai and holding out a perfectly round white pebble to him.

'Here you go, warrior. Anyone ever tries to hurt you again, just throw this at them and it will kill them.'

He nods solemnly, believing her, and clutches it hard until his knuckles go as white as the stone in his fist.

When she stands up she doesn't even look at you. Slips her hand into her bag and pulls out another cigarette, turning her back on the breeze and cupping her hand over the end to light it. You catch the scent of fresh-lit cheap tobacco and inhale hard. She starts walking away and you watch the loose swing of her legs, the way she holds her hair with one hand, and the cigarette with the other.

Cai is whining and you realise you've been squeezing his hand too hard, and even as you say sorry he is grinning and hugging your waist. Clouds are scudding over the blue sky. You're both shivering. The dog is nowhere to be seen.

'Come on, Cai, let's get you home into a nice hot bath.' You scoop him up and carry him, his arms and legs wrapped around you, relishing the weight of him against you, the way he grounds you. As you breach the dunes the dog bounds past and knocks your legs. You let Cai slide down and hook on the lead. You are caught again between the tug of the rope around your wrist and Cai's grip as he plods behind you. Tethered.

Your mam is standing by the gate when you get back. One hand raised to shield her face from the glare, search-lighting the horizon with her eyes.

'I was just about to come looking for you. You're both soaked!'

'We went paddling, didn't we, Cai?'

He doesn't concur, just holds up the white pebble and whispers, 'Look what Morgan gave me.'

NO COMMENT

It's not the career I planned. Not that I planned a career at all. If I were to admit that the process of school and college was merely because I had nothing else to do, you'd smile, because you knew that before I ever realised it. You always reminded me that I could have done better, if I'd just tried. Could have used my degree. But I never even put it on my CV for most of the jobs I've had. History doesn't mean anything when you are scanning tins in a supermarket or wiping arses in an old people's home. But you told me it made me middle class, having that certificate in an envelope in the bureau drawer, despite the benefits I received while working to top up my income. Despite the fact I've spent half my time signing on and not working at all.

Middle class. Only you would use that term to describe me. To everyone else I am classless. I don't stand out in the crowd at the wrong end of the high street, and I'm not followed by store detectives in John Lewis. I can blend in with the smokers outside the pub or with nicely dressed businesswomen walking through town at lunchtime. In fact, I don't get noticed anywhere. I'm invisible. And I keep myself to myself, keep quiet.

And that's how it all started. How I found a way to top up my income with cash.

That's why I'm sitting here now on a hard, plastic mattress

behind a thick steel door with a tiny hatch that's filled with eyes every so often as I wait for the next interview.

That's why I'm saying nothing.

I was always the one my family could turn to when they wanted a moan. All those brothers and sisters and stepbrothers and stepsisters and half... and well, you know. You avoided the get-togethers because it was too loud, too confusing. Families are like that these days, though, and I've never known any different. When I watch the 2.4s on TV it looks like what it is: fiction.

So many of them, and sometimes I'd not see them for a while, a month or more. We were scattered, all over town, all different ages. Some working, some not. Plenty of partners and kids to fill the time. Birthdays and Christmases a cramped squash in Mam and Dad's front room, people sitting on the arms of the sofa, on the back, while gift wrapping gets shredded and paper plates bend and tip food down each other's necks. Always a laugh, always so bloody hot you wish you'd worn shorts and a vest despite the slushy snow or freezing rain outside.

But when there was a problem, well. Then they'd pop round. Kettle on and a catch up. And I was the one in the middle, the one they all let loose on, because I was the only one that never passed the gossip on, never talked about the others. I can keep a secret, me.

I don't know why, but I've never had the urge to spread gossip, to embellish a story and lean in to whisper about someone else's problems over a hobnob biscuit.

I listen, and I nod.

And I don't even have to give them any advice. Let them get it off their chest and remind them after they've screwed their tissues up into damp snowballs that they already know what to do. What they feel. And of course, I won't tell.

And I didn't. Never. And although they'd sometimes ask me, say, 'Did our Terry come to you last week? Did he say anything?' I'd just shake my head and turn to flick the kettle on, inhale the perfume or aftershave filling my kitchen and wait for them to offload. And it never crossed my mind, not until now, that they never asked me how I was. Not ever. Not like you always did. But we all have our roles in life don't we, in our families? The quiet one. The loud one. The drama queen. I was the invisible one, the one who listened. And that was fine by me. It's easier to let these things just happen than to try and stand out, to try and be something else. I wish you'd understood that.

I put up a card in the shop window. Small, pale pink, with an invitation gouged in thick pencil. It didn't even look like my handwriting, the block capitals so different from my usual round letters. I offered a chance to talk, for a donation. A chance to tell a secret and know it wouldn't be spread around the town like the chip papers and cans on a Sunday morning. I can't even remember having the idea, and I don't think I was expecting to get an answer.

The first time the mobile went and it said 'Unknown Caller' I assumed it was one of those cold calls, my data sold on to the automated voices that no one in their right mind would listen to for more than half a second before hitting cancel on the screen. But when I answered there was definitely a real person there, a real cough and intake of breath before a voice asked if I was the Secret Keeper. It made me feel special the way she said it. A title. I felt a thrill run down my sides and settle underneath me as I sat at the kitchen table. I told her my address and she came round half an hour later. She knocked like a policeman on the front, like I might be deaf or something, and bowed her head and scurried when I called her down the side of the house to come in the back way. I don't use the front anymore. Not since you left.

She seemed embarrassed when I offered her a cuppa, stood by the sink looking around until I asked her to move so I could fill up the kettle. But as soon as that cup was in her hands, she let it out.

'I let him cry.'

I sat opposite her and waited, my own cup warming my hands. After a minute she coughed and carried on.

'I let him cry and didn't go to him. I don't usually do that, even though the books say it's okay. I think it's cruel.'

I nodded. I didn't need her to tell me who or what she was talking about. It doesn't matter, does it? It was the fact she was talking that counted. And I listened.

'I just knew though, that this time, if I went to him, this time I'd shut him up.'

I reached for a fresh packet of biscuits and used an invisible nail to slit open the plastic between the first and second disc. I held it out and she shrugged her shoulders and shook her head. I ate one. I know I'm supposed to be cutting down on sugar, trying to drop a few pounds, but as you always said, I've got no willpower.

'I knew,' she sniffed, and I could see that she was tearing up, that she was getting snotty. I got up and fetched a toilet roll from the loo and handed it to her. She pulled off a few squares and wiped her nose. 'I knew I'd stop him. That I'd just grab him and shake him and shout at him till he shut up.' The last two words ground out between clenched teeth.

The toilet paper was an angry ball in her white fist. She looked me straight in the eye. 'That's why I didn't go to him. I feel like shit, like the worst mother in the world because I couldn't hold him when he needed me. Because I stood in the garden and wanted to kick the heads off the roses and because it was ten minutes before I could go back inside and do my job properly.'

I nodded. I let her know with that tiny gesture that it was okay, that she already knew it was normal, that she did the right thing by walking away. I said it all without even saying a word, patting her hand instead, nodding every time she needed me to.

She sighed and got up, her tea unsipped. When she got to the door she reached into her handbag and handed over a crisp twenty-pound note, then walked away with her head up. I don't think she made eye contact once.

I looked at the money and smiled, did a little skip as the door closed and I twisted the key in the lock. I didn't have to declare it. No tax, just money. I shoved it under that Disney clock you gave me one year for my birthday, up on the high shelf, and tried not to smile too hard at the triumph.

After that it slowly built up. A few days of nothing then

two calls in one day. Followed by a knock at the door. I don't know what I was expecting, if I thought that people would come and confess to affairs and fraud, but I wasn't surprised by any of it. By the smallness of what they had to say. By the man who told me he still sucked his thumb when his wife wasn't there. By the woman who told me she had hit a rabbit with her car by accident, stood over its scrabbling front half as its broken back legs were dragged across red streaked tarmac. Eventually stamped on its neck. Twice. Actually, I think that one was the worst. Yeah, some people told me about their affairs, about fancying their brother's wife or giving blow jobs to some bloke in a pub toilet when out with the girls, almost like they were boasting, like it wasn't a secret at all, but telling me was a way of reliving the excitement. But most of it was small. Little bits of themselves that they couldn't tell anyone else. The dirty bits that couldn't be laughed off over a few drinks with their mates or charted on a whiteboard by a marriage counsellor.

There was one woman who pushed a screwed-up fiver into my hand and all she said was 'I ate a Mars Bar yesterday.' It took two minutes, less. She didn't even come in, just stood on the doorstep and leaned in close, like she was going to kiss me. Her breath smelled of boot polish. But the money added to the pile under the clock. And at the weekend, when I'd sent off fifteen more job applications for jobs I couldn't do and didn't give a shit about, I'd take five pounds and nip to the supermarket two streets over and buy a bottle of wine. Not to share. Just for me. Out of the money I collected for being quiet. I'd sit in on the Friday night and listen to a CD, holding a glass of something red and 'on offer' in one hand and my chin in the other, thinking about you. About all the times you asked me what was wrong and all the times I said 'Nothing.' About how you never believed me. I'd sing along a bit sometimes, smiling or nearly crying depending on the song, and how much I'd drunk already.

And then I got the job in the supermarket. Not Waitrose, nothing that fancy. Just Morrisons. Close, easy to do a split shift if I was asked, and it's not like I had a successful relationship or any kids to come home to, so I always said yes, and so they always asked.

Nothing makes you more invisible than sitting in front of a stream of people at a checkout. Invisible even to the people I knew. Even to the woman who the day before had told me she only changed the bed sheets once every two months, used Febreze every week so her family thought she gave a shit about the house. Even she never recognised me. She'd sat at my kitchen table, opposite me – just like at the checkout, but with two cups of tea and a packet of bourbons between us instead of a conveyor belt full of teabags and crunch creams. She'd almost asked me a question. I'd seen it in the slight twist of her lips, once she'd got what she wanted and could relax, dunked the biscuit into the cup and leaned back, absolved. But she didn't. She'd just reached into her purse and then made some excuse about not having any cash.

'It's a donation, right?' she'd asked. 'Not a set fee?'

The way she'd dropped a few coins by her empty cup and biscuit crumbs as if she was tipping the staff at a shit chain pub with the scrapings from her designer purse disgusted me more than her laundry habits. £2.37. But she was right. A donation. And I kept my word. And despite the irony of watching a bumper pack of Daz washing powder beep past me, I didn't make eye contact, didn't remind her who I was. Let myself stay in the background as she pulled out a gold card and paid the £176.89 shopping bill without a flicker of acknowledgement.

Not everyone ignored me though. I was walking home once in the middle of a split shift, planning cheese on toast and the midday episode of *Neighbours* for lunch, when a woman actually crossed the road to avoid me near the building development, where they are turning the old church into flats. I didn't recognise her at first, frowned at the sudden movement as she stepped out, almost into the path of a car, and scurried off up the road. It was in that moment when she had to pause to let the car go past that our eyes met and I could see she was scared, thought I might greet her. But I didn't. I keep my word. What's said is said and what's done is done. I glanced away first to let her know her secret was safe with me.

I guess I'm trying to show you I am good at something, even if that something is nothing. I'm so good at not talking I'm finally someone.

I guess I let it go to my head, holding all those secrets. Knowing, as I walked around town, the kinds of things people hold inside, the things that burn them up and won't let them relax at night. The things that need to be said just to make them smaller. The kind of thing I don't have. The kind of thing you wished I did.

I didn't notice the little boy at first.

When his mum called, she never said she'd be bringing her kid in tow, and when I leaned around the end of the house to call her round the back he must have been standing round the corner or something, because it wasn't until she was inside and still holding the door open that I noticed him. She asked if he could have a biscuit and watch telly in the other room while we talked. She spoke as if we were friends, but not close; as if we knew each other through work or something. Smiling down at him as if everything was normal. I led him through into the lounge and put CBeebies on. He unwound his scarf and pulled off his gloves and gave me a withering look, which was pretty impressive considering he looked about five, then grabbed the remote and switched it over to CITV, jumped back into the cushions and ignored me. I followed his lead and shut the door between the kitchen and the lounge, muffling the sound of some stupid kid's drama into insignificance. She was already sat in the hot seat, as if she'd been here before. But I knew she hadn't. I would have remembered.

And the thing is, she didn't tell me anything different to what a load of other women had told me over the months. She said she sometimes wished he'd never been born.

Nothing new there.

She loved him, she was glad she had him, but she occasionally thought about what life would be like without him, what her career could have been without the year off and the missed promotions. Like no one else had ever had the same doubts over being a mum. Not that I knew from experience. Not that I'd had the bitter pleasure of morning sickness or a career. But I'd heard enough women, and men, sit at my table and confess to regretting, even if just for a second, having a child. When they were tired, skint, couldn't handle their kids' attitudes, angry at their teenagers being such selfish little pricks. If only I could list all the other people, some of whom she might know, who'd shared the same dark secret over the pine circle of my kitchen table.

It didn't last long, she was up and ready to leave almost as soon as she'd offloaded. That was the usual routine. Once the words came out, went from thoughts that buzzed around in black circles inside your brain, like an empty milk bottle full of flies, into sounds, it felt better. It was a release. Just hearing yourself talk out loud is enough, I think. But I hoped they wouldn't realise it, start confessing to the mirror instead of handing over cash with their guilt in my kitchen.

She gave me a tenner, seemed a bit embarrassed as she looked around at the painted yellow woodchip wallpaper and cheap Ikea prints held up with nails, at giving me so little. She called him then, some middle-class name to match her shoes, and he came through rolling his eyes and followed her out. Neither of them had even taken off their coats.

And I didn't make the link at first.

When two days later the man banged on the door after a quick text asking if I was free. When he smirked at me across the teapot and asked for coffee, still wearing his leather driving gloves and winter coat, never taking them off. I'm used to people trying it on, coming up with stupid confessions to try and make me blush. Most of them do it over the phone. But I haven't changed the number because I can't be bothered to make another card for the shop window, and besides, it would only start again.

When he started by telling me about his car, and the bald tyres, and how it was illegal, and he knew it, but he hadn't changed them.

And then he told me why.

I didn't need to read the papers to make the link. Didn't need to put the TV on and see her puffy-eyed face pleading the same words you always hear when a kid goes missing.

Please, if you know where our beloved son is, please let him come home. We love him very much.

Really? No, we know you do, love. Saying you wished he'd never been born is normal, trust me.

I bet those feelings of guilt for even thinking it are killing her now. Let alone knowing she made them into sounds, let them fly out of her mouth and wing their way around my kitchen and the only thing stopping him hearing was the drone of a cartoon on the box.

And I knew he wasn't trying it on, trying to push me into reacting. I knew from the way the smile was gone and replaced by the kind of hard line you see on the lips of mug shots, in a line-up or something. I knew from the tone of his voice, the jokiness all drained out, the way he nearly whispered. The way he looked at me, trying to suss me out. Would I tell?

I sat opposite him, staring over the scarred wood of the table my sister had handed down to me, running my fingers over the dents made by my niece's knife and fork when she'd been strapped into a highchair, crashing cutlery and screaming. I tried not to think of her as I let him continue.

'I saw him come into your house. With her.'

He waited a minute, and I did too. I wasn't here to chat. It was his job to do the talking, mine to listen. I wasn't going to start handing out advice, because if I did, they could come back and blame me if it all went wrong. They talk and they work it out themselves. Getting it out, off their chests, is all they need.

The man who told me he hates his wife's hair but will never tell her he does.

The woman who said she wished her mother would just die, because visiting her in the dementia ward once a month was killing her slowly inside.

They're not going to go out and demand a trip to the hairdressers or push a pillow gently and lovingly over their mother's face until the confusion is over. But some of them, some of them know they need to take action, and I don't want to be the one saying it out loud. The ones who just need to declare their marriage is over? I'm not telling them to leave. They can tell that to themselves.

So I just sat and listened, and he carried on.

'It must have been the way he walked after her. The angle of his shoulders. He looked older than he should have. I don't know. But I followed them. And then that evening he was outside on the lawn, and it was getting dark, and she was sat in the kitchen with a glass of wine before he was even in bed. I couldn't help myself. I took him.'

I poured more tea, not that my cup was empty, just for something to do with my hands. My heart was beating like I'd just run a mile, truth be told, and I didn't want him to see that I was getting scared, that I was dreading what he was going to tell me.

And I knew he knew I knew who he was. That's the hard part.

Most of the people who've come here and spilled their guts

over the table in a way even Facebook won't let them, most of them are absolute strangers. This town is big enough for that to happen. And to be honest, even if my next-door neighbour came over, I probably wouldn't recognise them. We keep ourselves to ourselves round here.

But him? I knew him. Couldn't remember his name, not all of it anyway. But you'd have got it straight away. Because he was one of those people who's always on a committee or getting their faces in the paper. And I knew him because he was the dad of one of my friends from school. One of those friends that last about a month or so but then you find out they aren't worth the effort because they only want you around to make themselves feel better, or slimmer, or cleverer. She was like that. I'd caught her slagging me off to some other girls while I was having a pee and she didn't know I was in the cubicle. Later she'd been as sweet as pie, and so I walked away. Never said a word as to why. I don't make a scene, me. Faded back into the playground and carried on being invisible and average while she came top of the class and got in the paper for winning a medal for something pointless like gymnastics or cross-country running.

And now here he was, her dad, sat opposite me telling me about what he did to that boy, and where the lad was now. And challenging me with his eyes to go running to the police.

I held his gaze.

Tried not to ask him why he was watching the woman and the kid come into and leave my house. Tried not to wonder if it was *me* he was watching, or if he had already decided to take the kid and was following them. Or if he was already wanting to talk to me. To confess to something else. To explain why his daughter had let any boy at school put their hands up her skirt, just because they wanted to, but would cry herself ugly in the toilet for the whole of the next break after they did.

We sat. The clock ticked on the shelf and the hands moved round that grinning Mickey Mouse face and got closer to the time I should be starting my shift, and I never said a thing.

You wouldn't have believed it. I thought of you while I waited. I thought about how you always used to say that I could never commit to anything. Could never give a job more than about sixty-five percent and that's why I never stuck at anything very long. I thought of you saying when you left that I could never commit to you properly. That if I didn't want to share my problems with you, let you help me, then I obviously didn't trust you and so we couldn't stay together. I remembered thinking, as you slid your feet into your trainers and wrapped a scarf around your neck, *what problems?* And then you were gone through the front door.

He left.

He just pursed those narrow lips together, nodded slightly, then left. But he paid first, pulled a white envelope out of the inside pocket of his heavy coat. He'd prepared for it, this confession. He propped it up against the teapot once he'd stood up, the chair screaming across the lino as he pushed it back with his legs. Then he walked out of the kitchen, and I sat there for a few minutes listening to that clock before adding the envelope to the pile underneath it and washing up the cups. I didn't even open it, but it was heavy. Clearly, he felt he needed to pay a price. And then I called in sick to work and sat with the curtains closed and the phone switched off and just watched the 24-hour news on the Freeview box until the knocking on the door got so loud I knew they'd batter it down if I didn't get up and answer it.

I went to open the back door, to lean and shout for them to come round, but there were two coppers there already despite the banging still going on at the front. And two more standing halfway in-between. I invited them in and said I'd make tea, but they just wanted to talk. While I sat at the table and listened to them asking about the boy and his mum, two of them were wandering around, and I said nothing. Not even when one of them came out of the lounge with a plastic bag that had a little blue glove in it. Not even when they arrested me.

The metal hatch opens and eyes fill the space, then the bolt is drawn back. They smile and ask me to come out, to follow them down a corridor of similar doors each with a pair of trainers or shoes neatly paired up outside.

So now I'm sitting in the interview room again, facing a plain-clothes woman over a scratched Formica table that must have had a million confessions spilled over its surface over the years. And despite her showing me the photos – the ones they found in the envelope on the shelf under the Disney clock you bought me – that show his body both before and after he died, despite that, I'm saying nothing. They've got all the evidence they need to charge me, the fingerprints he left on the remote, the mother's statement about coming to see me. They say they've already searched the garden and I imagine the state of the house, the silvery black powder on every surface, the blue and white police tape alerting all the neighbours, giving them something to gossip about.

They must be able to tell I know something. They must be able to read it on my face that I'm holding something inside. That I'm carrying a secret. But I won't talk. I mean, I have to be good at something, right? I have to finally give one hundred percent. You've probably seen me in the paper already, maybe it was you who gave them the picture of me to print, maybe even gave an interview about how insular I was and said how it's always the quiet ones. How you always knew there was something going on, but I never talked to you. Will you come back now, to ask? Visit me in prison? Would you believe me this time if I said no, it isn't me, never has been? Either way, I seem to have found my vocation, and I'm not invisible anymore.

She's getting angry, this woman across the table. This woman who less than a year ago told me she had walked away from her crying baby to save herself from shaking it to death. I wonder if she has made the link, or if as soon as she walked out of my back door the relief at telling someone else how close she got to silencing her one child forever let her forget. Let her go back to thinking she was the perfect mother.

I remember everything anyone's ever said to me, but I'm saying nothing.

That's the one thing I can do.

She leans forwards and asks me the same question, for the third time, through pale-pink painted lips. She has a necklace with a pendant on it in the shape of a child's handprint. It swings out from her blouse as she leans over.

'No comment,' I say.

HANDPRINTS

A knock.

Hard and authoritative. One that makes her heart echo its weight and urgency before she even gets to the door.

This is not the friendly knock of her neighbours reminding her to put out the bins, or of the postman bringing far-travelled packages from her mother; this is a knock that says danger in five sharp, hard beats. She feels it in her ribcage as she walks down the hallway, speeding up when she sees two black and white shapes behind the glass.

At first, she thinks it is the police. Tries to work out what might have happened. Another burglary on the street? A murder like the one on the news last week at the far end of town? If so, she can tell them she has seen and heard nothing with a clear conscience, because she only leaves the house to go to work, the shops or to do the school run, and keeps her eyes down when she does.

She grabs her headscarf from the bannister and wraps it hastily around her hair and shoulders. Opens the door a crack, sees two men – wide as sofas – side by side. They have radios, white shirts and black ties under body armour. Paperwork. Behind them the morning street is bright with sunshine. Red brick terraces, small front gardens, parked cars. Two women, neighbours on the opposite side of the road, stand smoking, only half pretending they aren't watching. A teenager slides by on a bike.

'Samira Panahi?'

She nods, reaches out to steady herself on the wall as fear weakens her legs. Realising too late that she should have expected this, despite the reassurances from the council.

'My name is Tony Yates, I'm a High Court Enforcement Officer.'

His foot is on the threshold, there is a camera on his chest, its glass eyes watching her.

She waits.

'I have a writ of possession order, which means I am here to evict you for non-payment of rent. You need to leave the property immediately.'

She nods again, determined to retain her dignity. But her throat feels like it is wadded with old clothes and soft toys, and she can't form a reply.

'Can we come in?' he asks, not waiting for an answer. A neat beard trimmed to hide a bulbous throat. She can smell him as he passes; sweat, deodorant, coffee. His colleague follows, shirt rustling. She shuts the door on the eyes of the neighbours, imagines they will still be there when she opens it next.

The men find the kitchen and the room seems smaller with them filling the space. Samira is suddenly aware of the clutter; dishes in the sink, laundry spilling from the basket by the washing machine. Walls pasted with pictures and photos. She's lived here nearly ten years, and it shows. Her cheeks burn. Since her husband left there has never been a man inside her home. They lean against the worktops, taking control of the space.

It is half-term, midweek. Her daughter is sitting at the

kitchen table, pens and paper spread out between the lunch plates. Halfway through a drawing of a castle for her homework, she places the felt-tip down carefully. Watches these two huge men with blank-eyed passivity. This is a skill she has honed at school. Silence in the face of threat. Words bruising her on the inside while her face stays still.

'I have nowhere to go,' Samira says. Hears the pitch of her voice waver, leans on the back of a chair.

'You should have received a letter, at least a fortnight ago, telling you that you were being evicted.'

'My children are here. Where can we go?'

A wail from the other room. Her son is not quiet, the opposite of her daughter. This boy shares his feelings in abundance. Sobs at bedtime, screams at the smallest injustice – the wrong cereal, a loose button, a glance.

'How old are your children?' the second man asks. He is older, crinkled eyes behind glasses. His voice is soft.

'Nine and five.' She goes to the living room, scoops up her skinny son and carries him back into the kitchen. At the sight of the men his cry crescendos, he buries his face in her neck and clutches her shoulders.

'Have you been to the council? Did they say they would help?'

'I did have a letter. And I did go to the council. They said they can't give me a home because I have a home. They said that I couldn't be evicted because of the children.'

Her daughter is watching her, assessing. Samira worries for this girl, the ways she absorbs harm, as if she already knows there is no point fighting back, resisting. She is like a vessel into which other people will pour their troubles. She will fill up until she herself cracks. She sits at the table, completely still, while the Enforcement Officers explain.

'I'm afraid that's not true,' the older man with glasses says. 'This eviction notice was issued by the High Court, so you have to leave today. Do you have somewhere to go, family?'

'No family. Not here. My husband is gone. I've lived here for years, always paid rent on time until my hours were cut.'

'What is your job, Mrs Panahi?'

'I work in a care home, in the kitchen. They changed my hours so now I am looking for something else. I work hard, I always paid my rent always on time—'

'And they won't increase your hours again?'

'They say no, unless I do shifts. I can't work evenings…' she glances at her children, 'the holidays are hard enough.'

'Do you have a social worker?'

'Yes.'

'And they're helping you?'

'No. They say I don't qualify. I work for six hours a week and they say that means I am not entitled to emergency money. But I can't pay rent and feed them. I will, when I have a better job. I'm looking. But I need to feed them first.'

The men look at one another; she sees the pity in their eyes, and it burns her stomach.

'We need to stay here. This is our home.'

'But it's not your house. And we have to remove you from the property today. We can give you an hour to pack the things you need for tonight – medication, pyjamas, documents – but you must leave.'

'But where can we go?' She hates the shake in her voice. Her daughter watches her, and the fear she must feel doesn't show on her smooth face, but Samira knows it is filling up her insides. Setting like cement.

'Have you got anything from the social worker, a phone number? We'll try and help you, but while we try, you need to go and pack.'

Her son has worked her headscarf loose, has a skein of her hair in his fist and is chewing and sobbing at the knot he has created. She finds the last letter from Social Services, tries to slide him off her hip but he clings to her neck, wraps his legs tighter round her waist.

'Here. You will see they are not helping me.' She hands over the headed letter and doesn't wait for a response. Despite the primal urge to resist, there is no point. They are right – this is her home but not her house – and although she has never met the landlord, she can imagine that he wants only money and cannot see her family as real people at all.

An hour. What can she pack in an hour? The council said they would place her in a hostel if she was actually on the street, but they also said the landlord couldn't kick her out when she had a small family and yet here it is, happening now, so perhaps there will be nowhere at all to sleep tonight.

She takes shopping bags from the crowded cupboard under the stairs, straining her back to bend while her son still clings to her. Walks past the tidemark of grubby handprints on the stairs and begins to pack pyjamas and toothbrushes, favourite teddies that they will not settle without, story books to soothe them to sleep. She stacks the bags by the door, wondering how she will carry so many. She doesn't have a car.

As she packs her son pulls things from the bags, throws them and screams. Tries to put other things in the bags, things they won't need immediately: a large plastic truck, a desk lamp, a DVD. Her daughter stands in doorways and watches, silent and judgemental, as Samira takes each unnecessary item out and tries to calm her son's temper with soft words and gentle hands. Her daughter doesn't step in to help.

Samira stops and sits back on her heels, feels a rising panic and almost sobs. After her husband left she thought she would crumble from shame and exhaustion, but managed to find a kind of quiet pride in working and looking after her children alone. This house has been her sanctuary, her lockable door. A space she can take off her hijab and bra, wear jeans and play on the floor with her temperamental son or paint with her silent daughter. The clutter of ten years is her comfort blanket. But since the letter she has felt – when locking and bolting the doors as soon as they walk in and when closing the curtains before dusk – the moment creeping closer where the defences might be breached. A knock, that's all it took in the end. She shouldn't have answered the door.

She looks up when the bulk of one of the men fills the doorway.

'Are you sure there isn't a friend who can help you? Take you in for the night?'

For a moment she considers calling her mother, asking for money so she can go home, but she dismisses this thought – her mother has no money, and it wouldn't be going home for her children, it would be uprooting them even more than this eviction will.

'Anyone? A neighbour maybe?'

She shakes her head, afraid to speak in case her voice has gone entirely.

'Okay. Are you nearly ready?'

She can hear a sound, like a giant wasp or boring insect.

'What is that?'

'My colleague is changing the locks. You need to be out soon, but you will be able to arrange with the landlord to remove the rest of your things in the next week or so.'

Move them to where? she thinks. She already knows she must accept them as lost.

She takes the last of the bulging bags into the hall. Unable to carry her son as well, he grabs at her skirt and nearly trips her on the stairs. Her daughter has bundled her pens and pencils together with a hair-bobble, is holding a pad of paper under her arm. She is already wearing her coat and shoes. There is sawdust on the threshold, a gleaming new lock in the door. It is time.

'Did you tell them what was happening? Will they help me?'

He shakes his head. 'You should go straight to the council offices, tell them your situation. They have to find you somewhere to sleep tonight because of the children. You won't be on the streets.' He is trying to reassure her, his voice soft, but still he stands behind her and guides her towards the door.

Outside the midday sun is blinding. The two women are still there, still smoking, still watching. A man in a dark jacket walks past and spits at the white van with the High Court logo that is parked by her gate. She checks her handbag one last time to make sure she has her purse, phone and documents. She has six carrier bags of clothes and toys, a son who demands to be carried. The weight is almost too much already.

Just as they are about to close the door she rushes back.

'Please, just one more minute?'

The bearded man sighs, glances at his watch, but the older man with crinkled eyes behind glasses nods.

'One minute.'

She leaves the children on the doorstep, hears her son wail but the older man must have stooped to calm him as the screech softens to a whimper. She takes out her phone and begins to take pictures: the marks on the kitchen wall beside the fridge where she has charted her children's increasing heights from the first time each could stand; the doodle of a tiger her daughter drew on the living room wall in felt-tip — faded black and orange stripes; a dozen images of the handprints on the wall all the way up the stairway that show the tiny fingers growing like leaves, dappling the ascent; and the scuff marks on the bedroom walls where her son has kicked out in fits of anger and left black rainbows of rubber from his school shoes in the cream paintwork. There is a copy shop on the edge of town. Wherever they put her, she can print these out and paper the new walls with them.

She pauses one last time in the hallway and touches the blown-vinyl texture of the wallpaper, then steps outside into a street that feels like it is widening and spinning away from her.

The door clicks shut.

The big man is taping a sign to the glass pane in the door, biting the tape between his teeth to make strips the right size. The older man helps her carry her bags to the end of the front yard.

'Can you manage?' he asks, although it's obvious she can't, unless her children each take a bag. She nods, head still high despite this indignity. If he is too kind she will cry, and then her silent daughter will lose any last shred of respect for her.

Her son sits on the curb and begins tracing the path of a colony of ants through the dirt with his finger. The women across the road are shaking their heads, muttering, and Samira can't tell if it's a judgement on her, or on the men who have turned her out onto the street.

The men walk to their van, pause to phone through that the job is done. As Samira begins to pick up the bags her daughter walks towards them, looks the big one right in the face and then kicks him hard on the shin. He yelps, hops, curses. Apologises for swearing. Her daughter stoops to pick up the rest of the bags and begins walking away, out into the empty road. Samira tightens her scarf around her hair, tucking it tight around her neck to protect against the wide-open skies, the breadth of the street, the feeling of air moving against her face. Turns away from the men to hide the smile that this act of rebellion has ignited. Her daughter walks straight-backed and silent, but her head is held high. Samira follows.

Perhaps she has sheltered her inside too long.

HOMING

The pigeons are already dead by the time he gets back.

He's taken two coaches, and a local bus that slowly unwound his adolescence in a series of half-formed memories that made his guts twitch and ache. The final walk from the bus stop up the narrow, terraced street and through the cutting has left him breathless. Not with effort. He's fit enough. Scrawny and loose-limbed. But with emotion. The kind that clogs your throat like you've just inhaled old dust.

He stops by the front gate and holds on to the rotting wood, feeling it give a little beneath his grip. A gentle squeeze and it might crumble. He can smell dog shit, hawthorn flowers, the washing on next door's line. He can smell home.

The front garden is tidy, unlike some of the neighbours'. His mam always did keep a sense of pride. Not quite scrubbing the front step until it gleamed and slowly bowed in the middle with wear, but weeding, washing the net curtains regularly. He can hear sounds from the back yard and pushes through, the squeak of the hinges new. Appropriate, he thinks. A little cry out.

He considers knocking but can tell she's out back, so tries the catch on the high wooden gate at the side of the house and steps through. There are no bikes leaning against the drainpipe anymore, but he has to step past stacks of damp cardboard boxes, black plastic bags bulging like they're going to split any minute.

'Mam?'

It's not his mam out there. As he walks down the long thin garden towards the noises, towards the pigeon loft, he realises what is missing. The last sensory memory that should tell him he's home. There is no beat of wings in the sky above. No circling shadows flitting over the grubby concrete and struggling grass of the back yard.

The smell is still true though, just. The almost sweet scent of wood shavings, the warm heat of the birds themselves. He pauses to inhale and blink away the risk of tears before stepping through into the yellow heat of the loft lamps. His nan is standing between the walls of perch boxes, each with its wooden gate slid back. A pile of birds at her feet. She wipes her hands on her apron and squints at him.

'What are you doing here?'

Not *Hello*, or *Giz a hug, lad*.

'Mam called.'

She reaches for the last bird, a squab just coming into full feather, pressing itself against the back of its box. Before he can get any words out she's got it by the throat and twists, dropping it onto the pile at her feet and looking around as if there might be another she has missed.

'There.' A satisfied nod as if she's just finished cleaning the front room, polishing all the little china ornaments before a guest arrives. 'Well, what are you doing standing there with your gob hanging open? Get a bin bag, while I get the kettle on.' She pats him on the arm as she passes, and he flinches. If she notices, it doesn't slow her down. She's shuffling up the path in her red velour slippers, muttering something about the weather.

He stands next to the soft pile of feathers and loose necks, and imagines what his dad would do if he could see this now. He's too late, by what? Half an hour? He wasn't expecting this.

In the kitchen his nan moves around as if it's her house, still, even though she moved into one of the little bungalows at the edge of the estate a few years after his parents' wedding. The kettle is on and she's setting the milk bottle on the table, a bowl of sugar with crusted brown lumps where a wet spoon has been dipped back in for another helping.

'Your mam's not feeling well.'

'Where is she?' He remembers to take his shoes off. The lino is cool through his socks.

'She's in the front room. Resting. Give her a bit, she's going to get going again when she sees you here.'

'She asked me to come, Nan. She asked me to help with the birds.' He sits at the table, his old place. There are still scratches in the wood where he used to bang his cutlery as a toddler. He runs his fingers over the grooves and feels grains of salt stick to the tips.

'You can.' His nan plonks a teapot down in the middle of the table and groans a little as she sits opposite him. 'The bin bags are in the second drawer…'

'I know where the bags are, Nan. Why did you…?'

'Don't start, Ben. I'm just looking after things. Like I've always done. Last thing she needs is to worry over them,' and she waves a thumb over her shoulder towards the kitchen window and the loft beyond.

He knows better than to argue. He's not too old for a slap, she'd say, and besides, it's too late now. He sips at the tea, too strong for his tastes these days, but still welcome. Something to do to put off clearing the loft.

'Are you staying long, only I'll need to think about dinner.' She says this as if he's an inconvenience.

'A few days. Help make arrangements and all.'

His nan looks put out, works her wrinkled lips into a puckered pout and sighs. 'Where?'

'Here. My old room.'

'I'm in there for now. She can't be left alone.'

'Well, she won't be, will she?' This is the first time he's ever stood up to her, and he's shitting himself even as he thinks *It's about time*. Bloody hell, she's half his size, what could she do?

'Until you leave again.'

That's it. That's what she can do. He feels the words like her hands at his throat, like he's one of the pigeons.

'I'm here now.'

'That's nice. I'm sure Harry would have liked that.' And she moves to take his cup away before he's even finished his tea. He doesn't resist. Harry. Her son, his dad. Who has the greater claim to what he'd have liked? 'Shame you didn't visit sooner, to see him. He'd have liked that more.'

The front room is dark. Curtains closed in an old-fashioned nod to respecting the dead, or maybe to keep the glare off his mam's hangover. The room is immaculate, was only ever used for guests and for special occasions: New Year's celebrations with sherry and party hats in front of the portable; Christmas Dinner. There's a wall-mounted flat screen over the fireplace now, seeming to hover like a spaceship in a room that hasn't changed in decades, that still smells of lemon Pledge like it always has done. Only now it has the musty funk of being unaired for days, and the smell of last night's gin seeping out of the body curled on the couch. The TV is on, tuned to 24-hour news, and his mam is not even watching it. She barely glances up at the sound of him coming in. It isn't until he speaks that she reacts.

'Hi, Mam.'

She's up off the sofa and squeezing him then, and it surprises him, as it always does, how small she is. It feels wrong that she is tucked beneath his chin, and not the other way around.

'Look at you. Look at you.' She's got his face in her hands and is crying. He shuffles and waits for her to let go and sit down, patting the settee beside her.

'I'm sorry I couldn't get here sooner. Work, you know.'

'It's fine, Bo. He knew.'

They sit in silence for a minute, and he looks around, trying to find something to talk about. He wants to ask about the funeral, to get a date he can schedule into his diary. He wants to ask her if she knew about the pigeons, if she agreed to the cull.

'How's Jenny?' Her voice wavers, tired.

'Good. She would've come too, but...'

'It's different now, isn't it? Both working.'

He nods and wonders how much of her grief is because she

hasn't got anything to do now his dad's gone. Then chides himself. Forty-five years together. It's only been a few days. She's bound to feel lost.

There's a tap at the door.

'I'll be going then. Call me as soon as you need me back, Rose.' His nan gives him a last, meaningful stare, and shuts the door gently, as if she's trying not to wake someone.

They watch the TV in silence until the same story comes around again. A flood somewhere down south, people being evacuated from their roofs. Then he gets up and goes into the kitchen for the bin bags.

As he lifts the birds one by one into the refuse sacks, their heads lolling in his hands and warmth still caught beneath the feathers, he remembers the first time his dad let him into the loft, the strict instructions not to talk loudly or run about. He was five. Before then he'd only been allowed to stand and watch from the garden, feeling the thrum of wings as they took their turns to circle the estate and clatter back down through the hatches. The coo-coo-cooing in their throats a soothing purr while he half-heartedly kicked a football at the wall, wishing he was inside, part of the flock.

When his dad finally did bring him in, he stood stock still while the birds rustled around him on their perches, listened intently as his dad explained the different parts of the room – the couples box, the squab boxes, the widow boxes. He watched as his dad tagged the birds and packed them, big gentle hands, into wicker crates, and then stood by the gate as the baskets were loaded into the back of the old Ford Cortina. A final wave as the car disappeared around the end of the road. He didn't dare go into the loft when his dad wasn't there, and didn't want to sit in the kitchen listening to Nan going on at Mam about what she was doing wrong. About how his dad wouldn't spend so much time with the bloody pigeons if only she'd do her hair a bit nicer, cook him a proper meal.

The sacks are heavy, and already there are small holes where the birds' claws are beginning to tear the cheap plastic. He ties a knot and wonders what the hell to do with them. He's sure you can't just pop a sack of dead birds into a wheelie bin. The odd sparrow, brought in by a cat maybe. But thirty-odd fat pigeons? Perhaps the local tip will take them? There's probably a rule against that too.

He goes out into the yard to breathe in some fresh air and check online on his phone for how to dispose of two bin bags full of animal waste and can't think of how to phrase the search. However he types it, his search history is going to make him sound like a psycho. God only knows what suggestions will pop up in the targeted advertising.

He's staring at the side of the house, thinking, when he sees the other bin bags, bulging and wet. Cardboard boxes bowed with damp. He slips his phone back into his pocket and goes over to investigate. He has to tear a hole in the first bag, the knot is so tight.

Clothes.

His dad's clothes. Jumpers and shirts, and a pair of braces that half slither out of the bag, their fastenings clattering on the damp concrete. He pulls them, feels them snag and has to reach in and follow their length with his fingers until he can release them. They are navy, with tiny grey doves woven into the elastic material. He shoves them into his pocket and resists the urge to pull out a shirt and bury his face in the fabric to catch a final scent of aftershave or soap.

He thinks of the widow boxes. The mating pairs separated so the racing bird would fly home quicker, get the best time. How his dad would always come into the kitchen first, before going down to the loft; as soon as he'd dropped the birds off at the race start, he'd get home and give his wife a quick squeeze before picking up the flask of tea she'd have waiting to keep him warm as he stood staring into the sky. Ready to remove the racing rings as soon as the birds fluttered through the hatch, to slot each coloured band into the racing clock and record the time while the tired birds nestled and cooed with their partners.

He loads the bin bags from the pigeon loft into his mam's car and drives to the tip. Doesn't tell them what's in the bags, just gently rolls each swollen sack into the skip for Non-Recyclable Waste. As he drives back to his mam's he feels the clip on the braces dig into his leg each time he changes gear.

'She's only trying to help.'

'But do you want her to?' He shoves another mouthful of mash and peas into his mouth and tries not to remember eating this exact meal week after week as a kid. Mincemeat in gravy, mashed potatoes, peas from a tin. It must be twenty years since he's eaten this. Back with Jenny he'd be drizzling olive oil over something. He takes another mouthful.

'It's her son gone. I know how I'd feel if it were you.'

'But she's taken over already. You know about Dad's pigeons? Did she even ask you?'

His mam looks down at her own plate and pushes peas around in her gravy. 'No. And I'm not happy she did that. It was... cruel.'

'She is cruel. She always has been.'

'Don't talk about your nan like that.'

They eat in silence, listening to the kitchen clock mark out the time. When he's finished he resists the urge to pick up his plate and lick it clean, like he did as a child.

'What do you want for pudding, Bo?'

'Nothing, Mam. I'm good. Have you got a date yet?'

'Be a few weeks, the vicar said. Maybe just one week. He's coming by tomorrow.'

They clear the table and he washes up while his mam goes back to the front room and watches the news. Perhaps the looped footage of ecological disasters and terrorist attacks makes her own situation feel smaller, more manageable. He goes up to his old room and it has barely changed. Nottingham Forest football posters, a Count Duckula stuffed toy wedged onto a bookcase of paperbacks. Except it smells like his nan, lily of the valley and talc. He opens the window and leans out into the evening, inhaling the empty sky.

When he finally stretches out on the narrow bed he falls asleep quickly and dreams of hills and kites and wind, but not his dad.

In the morning he sweeps out the pigeon loft and takes the bags and boxes from the side of the house to the charity shop, careful not to look too closely at the fabric showing through in places where the plastic has stretched and is almost transparent. When he returns his nan is back in the kitchen, bleaching the tops and looking sour.

'Are you okay, Nan?' His instinct is to hug her, but not from experience. This is something he's learned you do since leaving home. Something he's picked up from Jenny's family.

'Fine.'

She means shut up and stop asking. Stiff upper lip. He wants to start breaking through, make a last-ditch effort to connect, to share the grief, but he just can't work out what to say or where to start, so when she tells him the yard needs brushing, and then to trim the hedge, he just nods, like his dad always did, and gets on with it. Calculating when he might leave without causing his mam too much disappointment.

When the vicar arrives he comes back inside, follows him to the front room and opens the curtains, the window too. Sees his nan's mouth take on the shape of a cat's arse. She tuts as they settle into the hard, stuffed chairs. The vicar has barely arranged his cushion before she starts.

'We want *The Day Thou Gavest*. If you don't mind. You do still do the proper songs, don't you? No tambourines.'

The vicar is younger than him, slightly tubby. Blinks. 'Of course, whatever you feel is right...'

His nan doesn't ask anyone else what they think. Just nods. 'Right. Good. Ben, go and make tea.'

While the kettle boils he checks his work email on his phone, texts Jenny. When he gets back into the front room with the heavy tray the curtains are closed again, and his mam is silent. If he stays he's going to say something, do something. It won't help.

Instead, he goes into the lounge, the cosy room at the back of the house, overlooking the garden. The curtains are closed here too, and the air is thick; the smell worse than the loft this morning, the lack of life tangible. The room is like two scenes overlaid: the old living room he remembers from childhood with its worn settee, TV cabinet and bookshelves stuffed with all those Jeffrey Archer novels and political biographies. But where he used to play, crashing toy cars into the skirting boards or hiding under the ironing board while his mam smoothed sheets and the room filled with the hiss of fragrant steam, there is now a hospital bed, an oxygen tank with the plastic tube hanging loose and trailing on the floor. The blankets are folded neatly at the end of the bed, as if ready for the next patient.

He walks around the room, touching things. The carved wooden hippo he was never allowed to play with as a child, a ceramic dray horse with a little leather harness and tiny gold chains, similarly banned. There isn't a speck of dust on either. He can't find anything personal.

He knows his father was managing. Still wheeling the oxygen down to the loft to tend to the birds, relying on a mate to come once a week to clean them out. He imagines his dad lying down on the wipe-clean mattress and watching the flock circling the house, the shadows flitting past the window every few minutes. Always coming back at night to croon to one another and snuggle safely into their boxes. He has no idea if his dad was happy enough to do this, or if it caused him pain to be laid up. He has no idea if his mam came and sat with him, or had already moved herself into the front room to watch her soaps of an evening. He suspects his nan has directed the daily rhythm of these last years, as she had the rest.

He pulls back the curtain and watches dust motes float in the light that floods in. He's not into old fashioned ideas like keeping the curtains closed until after the funeral, or wearing black just because someone has died. It's not about respect, he thinks, it's just something to do in the strange, timeless hours after someone has gone and before people expect you to move on.

He hears voices in the hall, steps out of the room and ignores his nan's glare as he introduces himself properly and shakes hands with the vicar. The man seems pleasant enough, talks generally about sorrow and loss, but has clearly never met his father. When the door closes behind him the three of them stand awkwardly in the hall, until his mam says, 'Friday. Next fortnight,' and pats him on the arm.

He's packing his rucksack the next morning when he hears noises in the back yard, a deep, gruff shout and a thump on the back door.

He gets to the kitchen just as his nan opens the door.

'Where the bloody 'ell are they then? What 'ave you done with 'em, you old bag?' His dad's mate. Come to tend the birds.

His nan lifts her chin up and stares him down. 'None of your business, and I don't want you coming round no more.'

'Bloody *is* my business! And you can't tell me…' He stops when he sees Ben come into view. 'Ey up, lad. You've grown.'

'Derek. Good to see you.'

The man nods and then looks back at the old woman defiant in the doorway. 'Where are them birds, any road?'

'I've dealt with 'em, and so you've no need to be here.'

Derek's face reddens and Ben steps in between them, gently forcing his nan back into the kitchen and closing the door on her. As they walk down to the shed, he glances back to see her watching them out of the kitchen window.

The loft door is open, and as they step inside they both hush their voices. Habit. It feels like it echoes all the same.

'I got here the other day. She was necking them. Mam called me to come and look after them, but I was too late.'

'Necking 'em? What for? They were good birds, perfectly healthy.'

'I don't know.'

They stand and stare around at the empty boxes and vacant perches. A feather blows across the floor.

'Does your dad know?'

Ben looks at him, and in the vacancy of the loft doesn't have to say anything.

Derek whistles, a single defeated note. After a short silence he says, 'The bitch. No offence, lad. Thank God he never had to see this, ey?' and then he pats Ben on the arm and leaves, still shaking his head.

'Go home, Nan.'

She's bleaching the tops again, moving things around to suit her. She doesn't stop.

'I am home. And you'll be gone soon. She needs looking after. Always has.'

It's time. 'No, Nan, she needs leaving alone. She always has done.'

She wrings the dishcloth out, twisting the grey fabric until it is loose and drooping, discarding it by the sink. He stands in the middle of the room, resolved. He's taller than her, what can she do? While she purses her lips and tuts and packs her handbag, he goes around opening the curtains, opening windows. The smell of hawthorn blossom, cut grass from the house three doors down, breezes in.

She shouts out before she leaves. 'I'll be back when you call, Rose.' She gives him a meaningful look. She will call, it says.

He follows her out, watches her from the garden as she pulls the side gate closed with a rattle. He turns away and pulls out his phone. The pigeon loft looks old, lichen mottling the concrete base, moss holding damp on the roof.

He listens to the phone ring, distant in his ear. A blackbird hops across the scrubby grass, tilts its head and looks at him with a yellow ringed eye.

'Ben?' She's answered. It takes a moment for him to clear his throat.

'Jenny, listen. I can't come back, not yet. I'm needed at home.'

He spends the day making calls. The hospital bed is collected, and then later the half-spent oxygen tank. He puts the commode at the side of the house, but on their side of the gate so the neighbours don't see it. By evening the room is almost as he remembers it. He finds his dad's glasses when he moves the side table and sets them gently on a bookshelf. It's as if he's just popped them there while he's nipped out of the room to check on the pigeons. The only thing missing is the beat of their wings, rhythmic and circling over the terraces.

When he's done, he fetches a chippy dinner and they eat on the worn old sofa, TV on low, the food balanced on their laps. Ketchup seeping through the paper, mushy peas grey-green and delicious. Vinegar. It could be 1989 again. He points out that she can sell up, find a smaller place. Find a hobby. For a few hours they talk, tentatively. Every excuse rebutted by him. He doesn't hold back.

'If you move closer to us, you could babysit. If me and Jenny, you know...'

They won't. They've already decided, and it's okay. He feels the smallest twinge of guilt at the false lure, but carries on. The greater good, he thinks. He has to release her. His nan's had her hands on his mam's throat for a long time now. Not twisting, but firm enough. There's no Harry to act as a buffer anymore. Not that he was any good at it.

In the morning, over tea and toast, he thinks she looks calmer. Resolved. He feels a lift in his chest until she comes out with it.

'I think you should go home now.' She gets up and starts rinsing the teapot.

'I can stay, until the funeral. I've already cleared it with work.' His inbox is brimming. He can work from home, they've said.

'No, you get on home. I'll manage. And Jenny will come to the funeral?'

'Of course.'

He packs his rucksack again, taking his toothbrush from the mug in the bathroom, smoothing down the duvet cover on his old bed. How long did it take him to leave last time? He was twenty-one before he'd finally had enough, shut the door on his old football posters and kissed his mam goodbye. His dad had been in the pigeon loft. Wasn't a hugger. Didn't come out to say goodbye. Ben had stood for a moment, looking down at the shed, the loft lamps making the doorframe glow, and then walked to the train station. Downhill; easier than coming back. It will be easy enough to do that again. This time she isn't begging him to stay.

He's halfway downstairs when he hears her on the phone, can tell by the tone of her voice who she is talking to.

She drops the phone in the cradle and pats him on the arm. 'Thank you for helping out. For tidying up.'

He thinks of the weight of the sacks, stoops to peck her on the cheek. He's done everything he can, he supposes.

He takes the train back. It's quicker. From the window seat he texts Jenny.

coming home today

The carriage is half empty. A girl in wellies and a hoody is scrolling her thumb over her phone screen, earphones in. A young man in a suit is focussed on his laptop. Ben looks out of the window, seeking something to distract him. The stems of crops in the fields are beginning to strengthen, and the hedges are overflowing white with hawthorn flowers. He notices a hawk, suspended on an updraft over the fields, almost still. His phone rings.

'Hi, what time are you getting back?'

'Late. I miss you.'

'I miss you too.'

He thinks of her in their flat, the small square rooms they've made their own: the second-hand Ercol chair where he sits by the window to read, and where she can reach to rest her feet on his lap from the sofa; the painting of Whitby Bay they bought on their first holiday together; the way the kitchen utensils sit in a vase on the kitchen counter like a strange bouquet.

'What are you up to?' He needs to hear her voice.

'I'm eating toast and Marmite and looking out of the window at a man trying to parallel park an SUV in a space way too small for him.'

He closes his eyes and shares the view with her, the crowded street and the shouts and traffic, feels his chest pull towards it. 'Do you think he'll realise and give up, or…'

'He's just dinged the car behind! Can you hear the alarm?'

He imagines toast crumbs spilling as she holds the curtain back, and her laugh is a magnet. He smiles, 'Yeah, I can hear it.'

'Be safe,' she mumbles around another bite. 'Get home safe to me.'

'I will, I promise. Not long now, a few hours. Do you need me to pick anything up from the shop on the way back from the station?'

'No, I went earlier, just come straight home.'

When the call is finished, he holds his phone in his hands and flicks between the train updates and the map, tracking his location; a tiny blue dot on a black line, curving towards her.

When the snack trolley clatters through, he fumbles in his rucksack for his wallet, and snags the catch of the braces. Pulls them out. Worn elastic and silver clasps, little tiny doves woven into the fabric.

SEVEN TEETH

Even though it's overcast and drizzling he visits: a flap and rustle, a clumsy landing, something in his beak. She leans against the flaking doorjamb at the back of the house and waits, cardigan pulled tight, patient. He hobbles towards her, not too close, and places a small white object on the cracked flagstones. Hops away again with a limp to cackle at the smaller birds and take his place at the feast. Each morning she spreads seeds and grains on an old tea tray on the rusted garden table for the birds. It's become their little routine: the food from her, the offerings from him. The jackdaw's occasional gifts started after his convalescence last summer, perhaps a kind of gratitude for the old rabbit hutch she had turned into a floor level shelter, the food and water and low, muttered words of calm while his foot and wing healed.

She waits until he is eating, watching her with a midnight-white eye as he bobs and swallows, then she reaches to pick up his latest gift. Pearlescent and smooth with a jutting ridge on one side and a neat edge the other. A tiny child's tooth, not yet yellowed by time away from a wet pink gum. A faint crust of blood sits deep in the crater.

'Where did you find this, I wonder?' she whispers, and amid the chuckling group of grey-hooded corvids, cooing wood pigeons and sharp-tongued sparrows competing for the grains, she's sure he looks up at her for a second.

Back inside the house she takes the tooth upstairs. The back bedroom is her hobby room, the space where her sewing machine sits mid-project, material unfurling from its mouth in a colourful waterfall. Strips of felt and boxes of buttons spill unchecked across surfaces – everything exactly where she left it. This is a room of shelves and drawers. Of miscellanea rescued and minutiae curated: there is a row of tiny skulls found in the pellets of owls, carefully cleaned and displayed beside an ornate time-tarnished buckle she dug out of a grass verge by the edge of town last year. Delicate sprigs of pale green lichen, wind-stripped from a wall and rescued from the feet of rushing shoppers, adorn the windowsill. They sit alongside seashells and smooth pebbles. She is a collector of curios, 'a witch' she's heard the local children whisper. The price you pay for living alone, for wearing long skirts instead of jeggings, for valuing the old skills of slow hand-eye coordination and shunning the digital rabbit-hole. She doesn't really care, is happy to walk through the park and be the only one picking up perfect pinecones instead of staring at her phone or posing for selfies. She sees the things they don't, the green and black spiralled snail shells stuck to mossy walls, the tiny shards of pale rose quartz on the gravel path. She knows the birds' first names, their old names: Margaret Pie and Jenny Wren, Thom Tit and Martin Snipe, Yellow Molly…

She has a special place for Jack Daw's gifts: a wooden tray of tiny compartments, slowly filling with his idea of treasure. Small broken toys from Kinder eggs, shiny bottle tops, blue and green sea-glass, a bright shard of blood-red transparent plastic that must have been found at the site of a car accident; a remnant of brake-lights crushed. He's a scavenger of debris, but every trivial item is a message to her, and the least she can do is value it.

She rolls the tooth around between her thumb and forefinger. This isn't his usual kind of gift, though. Usually he brings her forgotten things, useless things. But teeth are precious, swapped for coins by loving parents, kept in tiny tins or pretty boxes with locks of hair and baby's first shoes, surely? She stands by the window and peers through the trees at the neighbours' gardens, stripped and bare and decked with painted wood or patioed over. There are plenty of children who could have lost this, perhaps while playing. Maybe they didn't even notice until later, got their money anyway. She lays it in the next free compartment, loves the way the pale enamel glows amid the dark-stained wood of its new home. She has work to do though, can't lose time playing with trinkets. She settles at the treadle sewing machine and falls into a gentle rhythm, neat seams the reward for her time and precision.

Two weeks later – after receiving an ancient ring-pull from an old drinks can, four small beads that match (she imagines a cheap plastic bracelet snapping, the colourful beads zipping through the air and slipping down through blades of grass to where only he would find them), and a hairgrip with a tiny pink bow glued to the shaft – he brings her another tooth.

It's hot, late spring, and she has soaked the grain to quench the thirst of the visiting birds, mixed it with raisins that are now plump and juicy as fat grubs. She's sitting on the backstep drinking orange juice, savouring the sourness. He hops close, his knuckled foot tipping him slightly off kilter. Bows down and places the gift gently before dancing back in his asymmetric way and watching her, head tipped, until she reaches for it. The first was an incisor, this is a molar. Small, but solid, with four smooth corners and a deep cratered top. She strokes it, presses her thumb deep into the crevice until it nearly bleeds.

Her mind flits to thoughts of neglect, or murder.

She examines the tooth again for signs of damage or dirt, trying to push the image of a little shallow grave aside. But it is neat and clean as if polished ready to present to the tooth fairy herself. She listens, through the sound of birdsong and leaves rustling, to hear if there are children playing out, on the park in the corner of the estate or in their gardens. Realises after a few minutes that it is a school day, that they'll all be locked away in stuffy classrooms learning to calculate or create the perfect fronted-adverbial phrase. She places the tooth in the next free slot in her wooden tray and tries not to think about where it came from.

Four more teeth arrive over the next few months. She questions him and gets only his white-eyed stare in reply. In the evenings she drifts into her hobby room and slides out the drawer of miniature tokens, picks the teeth up one by one and rolls them in the palms of her hands before replacing them. With each enamelled gift she becomes more distracted, making mistakes in her work, seams drifting between the foot and the feeder mechanism of her sewing machine, knots tangling in the cam housing. She pricks her fingers when felting, the wool rusting with blood.

She bites her lip when Jack visits, wonders briefly if she's upset him somehow, unbalanced the order of things. Is cursed. Laughs and shakes the thought off for the nonsense it is before staring out of the window while a pan boils dry on the stove. Summer is here, the trees full and fecund. Fledglings begin their first forays to her feeding tray. She needs to know.

She is tending the herb garden by the back fence when she hears it: a musical muttering, like birdsong, but sadder. She pauses, her hands dirt-caked and the scent of mint and lemon thyme rising to perfume the air around her head, leans towards the rough larch panels and strains to hear. It is a conversation in only one voice.

—Why didn't you come?

—Because you are a bad girl. You didn't do it right.

She leans closer, searching the texture of the wood for a knothole or fissure. Peers through to see a girl, perhaps six or seven years old, with feral hair and dirty knees holding two half-naked Barbie dolls. There is a scattering of small trashy outfits on the parched grass beside her, half a bottle of sticky pink juice leaking into the dirt.

Ants are gathering.

One of the dolls has hornbeam leaves sticky-taped to her spine; makeshift wings already wilting. The girl waggles each doll in turn as she gives their sealed vinyl lips words from her own mouth.

—But I did it like you said. I washed them and put them out for you. It's not fair... you got them, and I got nothing.

—You need to be 'true of heart', like a princess. You are just a raggedy girl.

The girl lays one doll down and reaches into her mouth to wobble another loose tooth, eyes brimming. There is a shout from her house, her bulldog father telling her to clear up her mess, get her arse inside. She scoops the toys into a plastic bag, walks towards the house to a litany of criticism.

'Have you even brushed your hair today? Why can't you keep your clothes clean? Bloody hell, you're a disgrace. Get cleaned up before your cousins arrive, they always look nice—' the voice is cut off as the patio door closes.

In the sanctuary of her herb garden, she sits back on her heels. Birdsong returns to replace the harsh voice. She closes her eyes and breathes the scent of thyme and marjoram and raw earth, trying to focus on the soothing sensory details around her, but can't shake off the sorrow creeping into her throat like dry insects. Memories of her own girlhood surface, like a body rising from a dark lake: daily castigations for preferring to play in the woods rather than in the parlour; the vicious tug of the comb through her never-neat hair, tweezer-sharp comments from her slender, immaculate mother about how much more accomplished and well-turned-out her siblings and second cousins were. The weight of failure has taken years of slow detachment to shed, a carefully measured and maintained distance from her family finally allowing her to accept herself. A freak, an introvert, a dreamer. The jackdaws are cackling in the treetops, arguing maybe, over territory. She goes inside to hold the six tiny teeth, one by one, in her soiled palm. These weren't gifts, she thinks, more an invocation.

They are having a barbecue; smoke twisting through her trees, drunken voices rising and falling like a shrill machine, music blaring. At one point she hears a small victorious cry – 'It's come out!' – followed by a frustrated response. She watches from her hobby room window as the child is hustled inside, away from guests who might be disgusted by a triumphant bloody smile while they pile their plates with meat and swig beer. She shuts the curtains, tries to detach from their proximity. It isn't her place to interfere, she rationalises. And what can she do anyway? Arrive at their door to admonish the parents? Explain to them the damage they are doing? She cooks a simple meal but while she's stirring the pot she is dreaming of abducting the child, whisking her away into a forest somewhere and raising her as the daughter she'll probably never have. Setting her free. It's a dangerous thought. It hurts.

After the party has diffused, when it is quiet again and only the lingering scent of charcoal smoke remains, she goes out to stand by the back fence, watches through the split wood as the lights come on and go off in their house. Imagines the child carefully placing the tooth beneath her pillow.

But no. How could Jack Daw find it there?

She realises, barefoot and motionless in her herb garden, what it is she is waiting for. Eventually, as the moon slides high through the branches and the owls begin to call out to one another across the rooftops, there is the subtle click of a door lock. The child drifts out, ethereal in the half-light, hair sleep-mussed and feet bare. Through splintered larch she watches the girl pick flowers from the pristine pots by the glass doors, sees her approach the picnic table and make a tiny circle of petals, then place something small and pale as a jackdaw's eye in the centre. The girl stares at the sky for a while, then at the trees in her neighbour's garden, then goes back to bed.

She spends the rest of the night in her hobby room, sewing a tiny silk bag. Edging it with gold thread, hand-stitching a small blue flower to the front. As the first sliver of dawn ignites the birds, she stands in her kitchen and polishes a handful of pound coins with brown sauce and paper towels until they are sparkling. She has just enough time before it becomes too light to act.

Outside, she walks along the weed-cracked pavement to the gate at the side of her neighbour's house. It creaks, like a distant fox call, but she is in. Their garden is made of straight lines: neat lawn, box hedges, clinical borders. The only thing that seems alive is the small display on the picnic table: a delicate circle of leaves and flowers, a perfect white baby tooth resting inside a chrysanthemum head. She counts out seven shiny coins, fills the bag, and takes the seventh perfect tooth. It weighs almost nothing in her hand, and she keeps her fist tight so as not to lose it as she creeps home to soak the grain for the birds' morning feed.

It isn't much, she thinks, as she places it beside the others, seven tiny perfect teeth amid the lost things and trivia that Jack Daw brings. One night's sleep lost to sewing, a few pounds in a bag. She cocks an ear at the sound of an excited squeal from the other side of the fence. Smiles.

It isn't much at all: but it might just be enough for now.

THE WEIGHT OF A SHOE

He was driving in to work when he first saw the shoe, caught the flash of orange against the brooding green of the forest. His eye crumpled against a low sun. Something bright in the grey of the Minnesota winter. Something different. He braked hard and reversed, worked his unlit cigarette between pursed lips and pulled in to the mouth of the service road, bringing the car to rest beside a mound of gravel.

He sat staring through the windshield for a minute, letting the adrenalin from the rapid braking burn off. Then he shut off the ignition and listened to the engine cool. He checked his watch, knowing he had time to kill before work, checking just the same.

He needed air. As he stepped out onto the rough dirt of the pull-in he felt the pinch of his high-shine brogues on toes that longed to splay comfortably in his boots back at the house.

He thought of the house as he stretched the cricks from his back.

Thought of the repairs that needed doing, the garden going to seed.

But it was his at least, he thought. At least it was still his.

The shoe, an orange canvas sneaker with white laces, was on top of a mound of wet builders' sand that stood between him and the saplings struggling for light on the edge of the forest, displayed like a fishing trophy on a desk. Sam rocked on his feet for a few seconds, then reached into the car, inhaling stale smoke and the last warmth of the heater as he fumbled for his lighter. When he brought his head back out he could smell only the deep wet green of the forest either side of the road, the distant tang of the print works beyond the river, and his own armpits, already moist despite the chill on the air.

The damp ground was soft beneath his feet, with hard stones ready to turn an ankle if he wasn't careful. An access road beside the mound of sand led through the trees and disappeared into darkness. As he walked towards the shoe he tried to light his cigarette, but the breeze cut the flame down. He stopped a few feet away and lifted his suit jacket, ducking his head low to use it as a windbreak while he lit the tip. The hit of heat from the first drag as comfortable as a sagging armchair. He straightened up and used one hand to button his jacket against the wind that was driving up the road through the valley. Spring still had ice in its teeth. He was skinnier than last year; less hair on his head to keep him warm, less money to pay for fuel now he was paying alimony.

He turned his thoughts back to the shoe, to why it was displayed so proudly on the dark, wet sand. He'd seen work boots lost off the back of trucks, getting oily in the verges, the odd pair of sneakers hanging from a phone line where the kids had been messing about, maybe drunk. But never a clean shoe placed so carefully, so artfully, on a pile of sand.

He sucked nicotine and looked for the shoe's partner. Nothing obvious on the edge of the road, no bright colours amid the dark green and brown of the track. His Walmart suit trousers soaked up dew from the grass at the hems as he stalked at the edge of the forest, kicking at clumps of leaves and small shrubs. A truck drove past as he stood with his back to the road. He turned at the sound, as if guilty, to look. The driver must think he was taking a leak. He hoped it was no one who'd recognise the car, the second-hand beat-up sedan with someone else's NRA bumper sticker still clinging to the rear guard. Enough of those around, he thought, for it not to matter.

There was no other shoe.

He moved towards the one on display, noticed how dry it looked compared to the wet sand and dripping forest. Thought, *Huh*, and considered feeling it to see if it was still warm. But he'd read enough John Sandford novels to know that he could be contaminating a crime scene, incriminating himself by leaving his DNA on the laces. Skin cells in the wrong place, in the wrong State, could get you the chair. Or the injection. Or whatever the hell you got nowadays. He'd stopped reading the paper and keeping up with such things long ago – replaced them instead with novels where you knew the good guys were going to win regardless of the body count.

He looked around for footprints, clues as to how the shoe got to be perched so perfectly, but the sand was undisturbed by anything other than rain, its surface a moonscape of tiny craters from the drops. The shoe was clearly dry.

He finished his cigarette and was about to flick the stub into the long, wet grass, then thought better of it. Took it instead back to the car and added it to the dusty heap in the centre console ashtray.

The ride into town down the straight road did nothing to shake the unease from seeing the shoe. He parked in his usual spot in the lot and locked the car, although he thought no one would steal such a heap of junk, not even to keep chickens dry in a storm. But he locked it anyway.

Kathleen was already at her desk by the time he walked in the side door. He stood scuffing his brogues on the mat and seeing the streaks of dirt they left behind.

Evidence.

He unbuttoned his jacket standing in the blast of heat from the vent over the door, let his face unfurl in the warmth of the office. Kathleen was checking her face in the compact she kept in the desk drawer. Her hair was piled high on her head and her make-up was straight from the movies. She didn't look up to call *hi* to him, but as he sloped towards his office she snapped the compact shut with the click that punctuated his days at work, and rose to fetch him coffee.

He sat behind his desk and booted the computer, checked out the papers in his tray, feeling out of sorts because he was late, or later than usual, his routine broken. He stretched out his toes beneath the desk and thought about the pot plant wilting on the windowsill, the trees beyond bursting back to life, as he felt the leather restricting his movements. He thought about Kathleen as she walked in and placed a coffee on his desk.

'Makes a change for me to bring you coffee,' she said, reaching for the empty cup he'd left there yesterday.

'Leave it go, honey, I'll deal with it later,' he said.

Thought about her ass a little as she walked away.

Thought about the shoe.

THE WEIGHT OF A SHOE

The first meeting scheduled for that morning was with the Mattesons, a couple whose house had burned down just as the last snowfall of winter had set hard. He'd visited the property the morning after, seen it dark as a snowman's eye where the heat from the flames had melted the yard and turned the wood frame home to a heap of soot. The woman had been crying, had sunk to the ground and pulled a blackened perfume bottle from the edge of the wreck and tried to wash it clean in the snow behind the melt line.

'I just need something,' she'd sobbed, grabbing handfuls of brittle white ice and crushing it into the glass. Rubbing hard until her fingers went red raw and the snow was a grey slush by her soaking knees. 'I just need one thing to walk away with.'

Today he was going to sit them down and tell them they wouldn't get a cent to rebuild their life, despite their regular payments. It was an act of God, he'd explain. All the more rare for the time of year, for the weather.

He sat and thought about God for a while, then picked up the coffee and went back out of his office, back past Kathleen and the click of her mirror, and stood by the window looking out onto the Main Street. He heard his colleagues, Jeff and Leonie, come in and called *hullo* to them as they hung up their coats, sat at their desks and made small talk. Leonie was good at that. Weather, the kids, what she might make for dinner. She clammed up when something big happened on the news. Jeff huffed in response, replying in his usual series of breathy grunts and affirmations. Kathleen held them together like a mother hen, but one of them fancy ones. Ornamental.

He stared out into the street as it started waking up.

Shutters coming up across the way, people leaving the pancake shack after breakfast or with takeout coffee, striding to work. He looked at their shoes for the first time. Took small, painful sips of the still scalding black coffee and noticed how they walked. He wasn't sure if he was looking for someone hopping, someone limping with one bright orange canvas shoe tied tight and the other foot naked, or stockinged and cold. Avoiding puddles. As the crowd increased he watched for the uneven gait of a jogger, one leg slightly longer than the other, a stumble as one bare foot landed on a stone and hurt like hell.

He noticed for the first time how short the strides were of women in heels, how carefully and skilfully they balanced and lurched. How their unnatural gait drew the eye to the ass as they walked on by. Was that the reason they wore them? Or just an unwanted side effect of fashion? He thought of his ex-wife's walk, her fat behind swaying despite the wide flat moccasins she loafed about in. Thought about how he'd never cared that she didn't wear heels, that she was forty pounds overweight and gaining. It wasn't those things he'd loved. The memory of her leaving hit him like a heart attack, but duller this time. Duller every time. He didn't even catch his breath, just felt his chest tighten and guts loosen. He walked back to his office to deposit the half empty cup on the desk before going to the john. He had time before the Mattesons came in.

By midday he was on his fourth cup of coffee, standing in his office door and listening to Leonie talking about fuel prices and how it was going to affect her budget. He let her voice fill up the spaces in his head where a woman's voice was missing. Let her concerns concern him for a moment. He thought about fuel prices and global warming, about the programme he'd seen on National Geographic the week before that foretold a world with no oil, no resources left to burn except the planet itself. He thought about mentioning it but knew Leonie's face would close like a barn door in the wind, that he'd be hurting her by trivialising her worries against the bigger picture, so he thought about it inside instead.

At one o'clock he went for a walk. It wasn't how he usually spent his lunch hour, but stopping on his way in that morning had pushed everything off kilter. Most days he'd drift across to the diner for a plate of the special, share a joke with Madison who was young enough to be the child he'd never had. He'd eat and watch her dark ponytail flick side to side as she cleared the tables and wiped the counter. Her smile was like a sharpened sunbeam. Lovely and never really for him. It pierced his heart every time. He never looked at Madison's ass. Never.

But right then he didn't feel hungry, felt sick instead from the memory of Mr Matteson's tears, the way he'd choked them back while his wife just stared like a painting. Mr Matteson had been wearing dark blue sneakers. She'd been in canvas slip-ons.

Instead of filling his stomach he took his nausea for a stroll around town and tried to breathe some of the fresh air rolling in from the river. His shoes bit hard on his heels, made him conscious of his own gait to the point where he wasn't sure anymore how he normally walked. By the end of the hour his arches ached and his nose was dripping with the tight pinch of the breeze off the river.

He saw the flash of orange out of the corner of his eye on his way home, but didn't stop. Made a conscious effort not to look that way.

Back home he kicked off the brogues and microwaved instant coffee, sank into the armchair and sighed. He listened to the hum of the refrigerator for a while and thought about what to eat for dinner. The house was cold, but he didn't feel like hauling logs in and starting a fire, so he pulled on a sweater and his wide slippers instead, made himself a sandwich and settled back in front of the TV. This was how he spent every evening; dinner on his lap, flicking from documentaries to re-runs of old sitcoms and back. Soothing.

But he couldn't settle, felt the whine of a memory bugging him like a mosquito, no matter how many times he tried to focus on the plight of the bleached sea corals or the troubles of a made-up family in a made-up house. After a while he gave in to it. Had seen the episode a dozen times already and could relate the dialogue in his sleep. He went into the room he and his wife had slept in for nearly twenty-seven years and began pulling boxes and bags out from beneath the bed. He opened a few to look and rummaged for a while, feeling his guts churn at the forgotten items they'd once thought worth saving.

Near the bottom of a Target bag he found them. A pair of

her old sandals, the ones she'd worn all one hot summer and again in the winter when they'd holidayed in New Mexico. He held them in his hands and felt their weight, sniffed them.

They didn't smell of anything.

He didn't bother pushing the bags and boxes back under the bed, just left them on the floor where they fell. Instead, he lifted the blankets off the bed where he'd piled them the night before and walked out. He placed the pair of sandals by the door next to his brogues and settled down on the sofa under the blankets, like he'd done every night for nearly a year, to watch the National Geographic channel on TV until he fell asleep. He wanted to get to work on time the next morning, liked to be the first one in, to get the coffee going and have a cup ready for Kathleen when she arrived. The routine of making coffee for someone else, of measuring the grounds and listening to the cough and dribble of the machine fulfilled something in him he didn't care to acknowledge. He liked to see her smile thanks to him.

He'd already decided to stop at the service road on the way home from work the next day. Knew his evening would be easier if the shoe was gone, and the forest was all green and black and brown as usual. Or if he could look a little harder and at least find its partner, sit them both up there together, a neat pair. Maybe it had rolled into a ditch somewhere and was blanketed with leaves, or maybe it had been taken by an animal a little farther into the dark of the trees. At least a pair made some kind of sense.

He indicated and waited for the oncoming traffic to pass before pulling in and stopping the car. As the engine cooled, he walked over to the sand pile and stood squinting through his cigarette smoke at the three shoes on top of it. The orange canvas sneaker was still there, still in the same position. But beside it to the left was a lady's low-heeled court shoe in dark blue leather, creased around the toes and with the heel slightly worn on the inside edge. On the other side was a child's sandal, almost new. White with a yellow plastic flower on the bar of the toe strap. He stood awhile and breathed a mixture of tobacco and wet tree, damp blacktop and the stench from the riverside print works. He could hear birds in the trees above arguing over their territory, trying to impress the females or protect a nest.

Somewhere deeper in the trees he heard the sudden crash of a frightened deer. Just caught his scent maybe. He leaned as close as he could to the three shoes on the sand pile, screwing up his face in contemplation. It no longer felt like a crime scene, more like a shrine. A cairn. Isn't that what they had in Scotland? A pile of stones that travellers add to with rocks they've carried with them for miles. He tried to imagine the owners of the two new shoes. A lady with a hole in the toe of one stocking, a chipped nail peeking through maybe. A child strapped into the back of an SUV, crying over the loss of her favourite sandal.

There was no point in looking for the other orange sneaker. He shook his head and walked away.

He stopped driving past the pull-in. Took instead the longer route to work, looping out through the next small town, where a gas station that tripled as the local grocery store and café was the only commercial building. He stopped there once to pick up milk for the coffee on his way in, saw on the counter a baby's shoe beside the Hershey bars and packs of gum. He picked it up as the skinny kid serving him cashed up his milk and tobacco, thought, *Huh*, and put it down again. The mom would pick it up next time she needed bread, or beer. She'd get it back. It was a small town.

But after work one day, a week or so later, his old routine kicked in, the weight of the day enough to make him follow the old route home. He had no intention of stopping until he was already indicating. As he pulled in, he could see the pile had grown. He lit a cigarette and stepped out of the car, taking a moment to observe the heap of shoes on top of the heap of sand before getting closer to investigate.

It was a mass of colour and style. A beautiful jumble.

He stepped closer.

Counted.

Sixteen shoes and all them from the left foot. He'd not noticed that before, when there were just three, but now, as he took the time to look at each one, to visualise the possible owners, to wonder if he recognised any of them, if Kathleen would walk in the next morning on one high heel, or Jeff stumble through the office like he stumbled through his sentences, he could see they were all from the left foot.

A car hummed by, but he didn't turn to look.

He thought about the Mattesons.

He thought about Madison and her ponytail, her quick smile.

He thought about God for a minute.

He got back into the car and thought about his ex-wife sitting in the sun and wiggling her toes at the same sky he was still shivering under.

He drove home and placed his shiny brogues beside her old sandals and thought about getting a dog. Dismissed the idea within a second for the long hours he worked.

The next morning he set off early. Stood in the service road for a full ten minutes without a single car going past behind him. Two more shoes had appeared overnight, and yet no one was saying anything. He thought maybe Leonie might have seen, was sure she lived up this way, but maybe not as far as him, and maybe it was too big for her to talk about. Maybe she didn't have the words. Maybe it didn't matter why, anyway.

He stood in the breeze from the river and thought about her new partner, who he'd never met.

He thought about the kind of dog he would have got if he had the time.

He went back to the car and got one of his ex-wife's sandals from the passenger seat where he'd placed them earlier. Picked up the left one. Walked back to the pile and found a space to balance it near the top. He thought about that for a while too.

Then he used his right toe to push on the heel of his left brogue. Felt the laces tighten across the bridge of his foot as the heel crowned, and then the release as it breached. The shoe came off and he lifted it, dangling on his toes, to take hold without having to bend down. He put his stockinged foot back down on the dirt, felt the damp from the ground seep into the wool of his sock, felt each sharp stone embedded in the mud push into his soft flesh. He placed his shoe on the other side of the pile. Stood back and thought about it all for a while and then walked back to the car, his gait uneven and rewarding, getting feedback from the left foot that his right foot sensed despite its leather confines. He'd have to go over to Walmart later and buy new socks, new brogues to wear for the meetings and site visits. But for now, for a while, he could wriggle at least half his toes freely. He sat in the car and felt the clutch pedal with the ball of his foot. Pressed it a few times to get used to the change in pressure, in control, from having no shoe on his foot. Didn't want to get in an accident and have to claim on his insurance. He pulled out onto the long, straight road into town, changed gear and eased his foot off the clutch, and let himself go.

THE MESSAGE

Mother and Son are eating dinner on the sofa when she first hears the noise. A shrill note that cuts through the music and voices on the TV and stops her fork somewhere between plate and lips. A strand of pasta falls back onto her plate.

'Did you hear that?' she asks, but knows he hasn't. He is curled into the corner of the sofa, a cushion on his knee protecting his legs from the heat of the plate.

'What?' His eyes dance with cartoon reflections.

'A bird.'

He pauses between chews, holds the food in his cheek like a hamster and listens, but the sound is absent. He half shrugs and keeps eating, but Mother is on guard, eyes flicking over the piles of boxes that line the walls, the newly plastered chimney breast. Wind is vibrating in the flue. She begins to doubt she heard anything. She leans forward to grate more parmesan onto her plate and hears it again, a note of song or distress. She can't tell.

'How?' His question is as dissonant as the bird's call.

'How what?'

'How is it a bird?'

'Turn it down. I need to listen.' She gestures for the TV controls. Son always holds the remote in the hour before bed. He reaches beside him and drops the volume by one or two notches. It's not enough. 'Turn it down, now.'

His sigh is a cloud of garlic and frustration. She is leaning forward still, straining to hear. Twice more the sound rings out, two clear notes like a chiming bell, and now she's sure.

'There's a bird in the house,' she states, as much to hear her own voice confirm it as to share the news. Son's eyes widen and he starts to move. 'No, finish eating first. I might be wrong anyway.'

He sinks back into the TV show.

They eat, but Mother is still listening for the call. Each time she hears it she is less certain, more concerned. It must be a bird, but she suspects it has fallen down the chimney, is trapped between the new flue for the log burner and the blackened bricks of the original stack. She anticipates an evening of listening to it die.

As she chews her food she runs through possible scenarios in her head. This is how she has always managed things – imagine the worst, visualise possible outcomes, calculate probabilities, find solutions before you even need them. That way you can discard the rest, unused, but you never find yourself surprised. That was how she came to the decision about the house, about the move. She had already cried dry her worries about the new school and bigger mortgage by the time the contracts were signed. Now they just have to live with the consequences, eyes open.

When the food is finished, they sit. She is in no rush to clear the plates and glasses from the coffee table, to begin the hunt for a bird that will probably die, that will haunt Son's dreams of helplessness. He is sensitive to the suffering of animals. Cries over squashed worms and once over a dead rat they found at the bottom of the garden. She watches him and listens, hopes she's mistaken. There is a tree just outside the window, but she's never heard a bird sing there, not at half past six on a dark, wet night. And besides, the sound, irregular and plain, is coming from the middle of the house, from where the chimney tunnels through and provides a warm heart to their new home. Or will, when it's finished. She closes her eyes and tries to visualise a life beyond the dirty wallpaper and leaning stacks of boxed possessions, tries to see why they bought the house in the first place – the good school, the proximity to work, the south-facing garden that will one day contain flowers and not just mud and flagstones.

But the sound cuts through her thoughts and Son is bored with the TV.

'Can we look for the bird now?'

'Clear the table first, then yes.'

'Can we keep it when we find it?'

'We might not find it, there might not be a bird.'

'But you said!'

'I said I thought I heard a bird. We'll see.'

They pick up the crockery and balance it to carry it through to the kitchen. More boxes sit in the corner, and the floorboards are exposed where the plumber has been re-routing the pipes. Mother is already in her pyjamas, needing the comfort of loose soft cloth and slippers after the constraints of a suit and smart shoes. Son is still in his school uniform. She wants him asleep within the hour so she can drink a glass of wine and watch TV. She knows he'll still be awake when Father gets home though. He hasn't slept well since the move. They stack the plates in the sink and Son begins to rush towards the stairs.

'Wait, you must be quiet or you'll scare it.'

He drops to the floor and begins to crawl up. Mother listens and tries to gauge where the bird might be, still worried it is in the chimney. She hasn't heard any scratching though.

'How did it get in?' She isn't asking Son his opinion, but voicing the question out loud fills the gap between the ringing calls.

'Through a window?'

'They're all closed.'

'Through a hole?'

'There aren't any.' She considers this again. There are holes; gaps in the brickwork in the bathroom, an old boiler vent. But it is capped. She glances up to check that the hatch to the attic is closed, that the bird hasn't accessed the roof space through a broken tile or under the eaves and flown down towards the light. 'It might not even be a bird. It might be the batteries in the smoke alarm going dead. Or something from next door.' But she knows, even as she says this, that it's a bird. The irregular gaps between the trills, the way the sound has come from a slightly different location each time it has cut through their conversation.

The house has called out many sounds to them since they moved in: the hollow vibrating tone of the extractor fan in the bathroom that hums deep and loud when the wind blows over the roof; the whistle of air rushing around the corner of the plot and through the gap in the window of the spare room; the steady, heavy drip of rain water from the broken gutter outside the master bedroom; and worst of all the squeak of the loose letter box, rattling and swinging all night whenever the weather is bad. And here, this winter, it's been bad. She hasn't seen clear sky in four months.

But this noise is organic, is alive. They pause at the top of the stairs, balanced on the dirty carpet she cannot wait to remove and replace once the renovation is over. They listen, their bodies pressed together, and hear it call. The sound comes quicker now, a repeated plea. They have to find it. They are standing beside the chimney breast and it's coming from that side.

Mother opens the door to Son's room, hoping it's there.

Son tries to push through, beneath her arm, but she holds him back.

'Slowly. Look.'

On the bed sits a brown bird, twice the size of a sparrow, not as fat as a blackbird. It has vague speckles down its chest and she thinks it must be a starling, but when she searches the internet in the next few days she won't find anything that matches. Starlings have distinct white speckles, a petrol-green sheen to their shoulder feathers. This bird is dull. She thinks it must be a female, lacking the necessary flamboyance a male requires to find a mate. It perches on a mound of duvet, watching them through the crack in the door with a bright eye and turned head.

'Go in quietly,' Mother says, and opens the door a little wider. They slip through and close the door behind them. The bird takes flight, moves from the bed to the top of a cupboard. Mother can see white streaks and dashes on the carpet, the edge of a chair, the duvet. Son is walking towards it, hand outstretched as if he expects it to hop onto his fingers, to act like a character from a movie and speak to him. The bird is poised and watchful.

'Sit down and try to be still, don't scare it.'

But children can't be still. The bird moves around the room, hopping from the edge of the cupboard to the arm of the chair, dropping onto the floor and moving between toy cars and a wooden pirate ship. Son moves too, leaning and bending to see it from all angles, reaching out to it in expectation of friendship. Mother finds herself reaching out, holding him back. She is no longer sure who she is protecting, him or the bird. She is still trying to work out how it got into the house, into the bedroom. The door was closed, the windows are closed, and she searches the edges of the room for a gap they have missed, a hole through which it could have crawled. Its song is cheerful, insistent. It doesn't seem afraid.

'What do you mean, Mummy?' Son asks, breaking his gaze away from the bird.

'Huh?'

'You just said, "It has to mean something." I heard you whisper it. What do you mean it has to mean something?'

'Nothing.'

'It's not nothing, you said it, so must mean something.'

'I was wondering why the bird was here. I don't know how it got in. It feels like, I don't know, like a message.' She knows she shouldn't be starting this conversation, that he'll latch onto something, a detail, and imagine it out of proportion. But the lack of an adult to talk to, her husband to laugh off her ideas, creates a void he often fills. The bird hops closer.

'A message? Like carrying one, like a pigeon?'

'No. More like the bird itself is a message.'

Son turns back to the bird, but Mother can tell by the hunch of his shoulders he is considering this.

'It must have flown in when we came home, it must have come through the door when we did.' Mother is sitting cross-legged and feels her back start to ache. She wants Son in bed so she can stretch out and stop thinking for half an hour. She wants a break. 'We should let it out.'

'No! Wait till Daddy gets home. He can see it then. It's a special event!'

'Okay, but as soon as he gets in the bird goes out.'

They sit and watch. The bird doesn't move. It is beneath the chair, its eyes perfect circles of black in the shadow.

'I think it's hungry.' Son is up and out of the room before she can grab his trouser leg and restrain him. She eases the door closed behind him to stop the bird following. The last thing she needs is a chase, the beat of breaking wings on the walls and ceiling as it panics.

The bird is still. It watches her and she watches it. She whispers, *Why are you here?* and it cocks its head at the sound. It shrills a cry that makes her jump, makes her place her hand on her chest in surprise. Its voice is so much louder close-up. She can feel her heart fluttering beneath her fingers.

Son creeps back in, managing to contain his excitement in consideration for the bird. He sprinkles muesli on the bedroom floor, on the toys and discarded pyjamas, all the time crooning and trying to whistle to tell the bird that dinner is served. He whistles on the in-breath, a reedy, weak sound. Sometimes it makes him cough, as if the note has stuck in his throat.

Mother groans. She can add hoovering up muesli to her list of things the house demands, of things she must complete and fix before they can relax and just get on with life.

'Sit down!' Even though she whispers, it is through gritted teeth and so the frustration is hissed out, heard. Son sits.

'What kind of message? Do you mean like a symbol?'

Mother is surprised at Son's ability to make such a sophisticated conclusion at such a young age. He is eight years old. Thoughtful. She is often surprised at his maturity.

'Where did you hear about symbolism?'

'At school. Flags and signs. The swastika. That's a symbol. And the green arrows in a recycling triangle. But the teacher said some animals are also symbols. The lion is a symbol of strength, I think, so people use it on flags and T-shirts.'

'They teach you about swastikas at eight? I don't think I did that until high school.'

'So what does a bird mean?'

'Well.' Mother decides to give in, as she often does, and go with the topic. She's never been good at protecting him in this way, at dumbing down their conversations to keep him functioning socially at an age-appropriate level. 'Peacocks can symbolise pride, and some birds, like crows, symbolise death or doom. The Old English poets used animals a lot to show the outcome of a battle. So, crows and ravens eat dead flesh. They are carrion eaters. When a crow is used in an Old English poem it shows the battle is lost or something, because the crow comes when it knows there'll be food.'

'The dead warriors?'

'The dead warriors.'

'What about other birds?'

'Mmm. Eagles symbolise freedom, which is why America uses them a lot. Doves are for peace. You know that from the Bible stories, don't you?'

'Yes.' Son fiddles with a raisin, then tosses it towards the bird. It flinches and trills. Son's eyes widen.

'So what kind of bird is this? What does it mean?'

'I don't know what kind of bird it is. But what birds do can mean something too. Or, at least, superstitious people think so.'

'Like what?'

If Mother had looked at him then she might have seen the shadow of a frown beneath his thick fringe, might have caught the way he was fingering his sleeve. The first signs of anxiety. But she was looking at the bird.

'Like, some people think if you see one magpie it's bad luck, and two is good luck. Same with cats.'

'Cats?'

'You know, a black cat crossing your path is bad luck.'

'Is it? I like cats.'

'Me too. Especially black ones.'

'Why black ones?'

'Because no one else does, because they are bad luck. But I don't believe that. They are just cats.'

'So what does a bird in the house mean?'

Mother looks at her watch. Father is late. But then he often is now. She wishes he'd come home so they could show him the bird, catch it, release it.

'Did you know it's supposed to be good luck if a bird poops on your head?'

'Eeuw! That's disgusting. That's not good luck!'

'Still, that's what they say. And bad luck if a bird flies into your window.'

'Like this one?' He is chewing his sleeve now. The hem is

already threadbare even though the uniform is new, only two months old.

'No, I mean fly into a closed window, hit it. It's more bad luck for the bird though really. They get hurt or die.'

'Why would they do that? Are they trying to get hurt?'

'No.' Mother wraps an arm around Son and pulls him close. She can hear the distress in his voice now. She leans over and checks her watch, irritated at Father for being so late. Knowing it's almost certainly not his fault but wondering all the same if he chose an extra hour in the office over an extra hour at home. She has no such luxury. She has to do the school run straight from work. 'Birds fly into windows because they see the sky reflected there.'

The bird moves, hops out from under the chair and trills, twice, before flying up onto the bed. It looks down on them. Son shifts his position against Mother to see better. Holds out his hand hoping so hard that the bird will fly onto it that she can feel the wish through his clothes and her own, hot and lucid.

'This bird came for me,' Son says. 'Can we keep it?'

'No.'

'Why not? It came into the house, it wants to be here. It can live in my bedroom and be my friend.'

'I think it came in by mistake, though.'

'And what does that mean?'

Mother pulls her phone out of her pocket and searches online for superstitions.

'I really think I should keep it.' He is making a small pile of muesli with his toe, watching the bird for a response.

'No, it's cruel.'

'But it must mean something good. It's pooped all over everything. So much good luck!'

Mother opens a webpage and reads out loud from the small print on the screen.

'Here. Crows are bad luck, already done that one.' Her finger slides over the screen. 'Poop on your head is good luck... Ah, here we go. A bird flying into your home is a sign of an impending message or an impending death...'

'What does *impending* mean?'

'Coming soon. So, you might be getting a letter soon!' Mother's voice is cheery, but the false note wavers.

'Or I might die.' Son speaks in a monotone.

'You're not going to die. Anyway, it's all superstition. We don't believe in that nonsense.'

'Where's Daddy?'

'Just running late.'

'How do you know?'

Mother looks at her phone again. There is no reply to the text she sent as she was cooking dinner. *Do you want me to save you some?*

'He gets stuck in traffic.'

'Or he's dead.' Son gets up, startling the bird. It flaps around the room twice before perching on the edge of the wardrobe and pooping down the side. The white streak looks like a tear. Son stands at the window looking through his own reflection into the dark street below.

'What are you looking for?'

'Crows.'

'Come on, pyjamas.' She regrets letting the conversation develop. She should have kept it simple, cheerful. She should have read ahead to avoid burdening him with more worry, with gloomy imagery. She opens the bottom drawer of his dresser and pulls out clean pyjamas.

The bird watches them as she helps him change. He is thin, his knees and elbows bulging and bony. His long toes curl like claws. She thinks back to the dinner plates, the amount she had to scrape off his plate before she could soak it in the sink.

'Do you want some supper?'

'I'm not hungry.'

'How about a few biscuits? Some warm milk?'

'Okay.' He is back at the window, and she knows he won't do more than nibble the edges around until the biscuits are smaller, crenulated.

She eases out of the room, and is nearly at the foot of the stairs when she hears him call, 'He's home!' The relief in his voice is echoed by three shrill notes from the bird, as if it too is celebrating.

Mother feels tension slip from her shoulders as she opens the fridge and pours milk. Father brings a rush of cold air when he opens the front door, the squeak of the letter box as he closes it again.

'The traffic is murder,' he announces. 'Did you save me some food?'

'In the oven.' Mother kisses Father in relief, with passion. His arms are trapped by the sleeves of his coat as he tries to shrug it off, and she lingers on his lips. 'You'll never guess what we've got upstairs.'

They walk up together, carrying biscuits for Son. There is a slight mishap at the bedroom door as they try to squeeze through, and milk is splashed on the carpet. It doesn't matter because the carpet will be replaced when the renovation is completed.

Son tells Father about the bird, about how being pooped on is supposed to be good luck and now he has the luckiest bedroom in the whole of the world because, look, there is poop everywhere.

Slowly, they persuade Son that the bird needs to go home to its family. That somewhere its partner and babies (the time of year is forgotten for convenience) are waiting for it. As they open the window a chill flutters in, bringing gooseflesh to their arms. They spread out, hands held wide, and slowly back the bird into the corner, forcing it towards the open window. Downstairs Father's phone starts ringing, and when the bird calls out they laugh, and say it must be replying, it must think the phone is another bird. The bird hops onto the sill, turns to face them. They can see themselves in the reflection of the window, arms wide and flapping, like three puppet birds. It drops away, outside, out of sight. Mother shuts the window and Son presses his nose to the glass to see where the bird has gone.

'Get your teeth brushed. Bedtime.' Mother ruffles Son's hair, moves towards the stairs to find out who is calling Father at this hour. When she glances back she can see his face reflected in the window, fading behind a circle of breathy mist.

ACKNOWLEDGEMENTS

Gratitude first and always to Simon and Xandr, for the inspiration, patience, feedback and encouragement to keep writing and rewriting. This is your book as much as mine, and I love you both fiercely.

Two others have been vital to the honing of these stories: my friend and colleague Dr Mel Ebdon, whose expert literary advice has saved me much embarrassment and whose company is always a joy; and my editor at Parthian, now also a cherished friend, Carly Holmes, who brings both a critical eye and a writer's heart to her work, and has helped me make these stories into a collection.

Thanks also to all the other writers and friends over the years who gave advice, feedback and encouragement, and to the publishers listed below who sent some of my stories out there into the world and gave me the confidence to keep writing.

A final thanks to Mortimer, for all the walks that helped me think.

***

'A Cloud of Starlings' appeared in *Take a Bite: The Rhys Davies Short Story Award Anthology*. Cardigan: Parthian, 2021

'Beached' was chosen for the final edition of Ellipsis Zine, *Swansong*, 2024

'Un/determined' appeared in *The Fish Prize Anthology 2017*. Bantry: Ireland.

'A Sudden Rush of Air' was a *Litro Story Sunday* feature in 2017

'No Comment' appeared in the *Dinesh Allirajah Prize for Short Fiction: Crime Stories*. Manchester: Comma Press, 2022

'Handprints' was written for the Narrative Research Group Anthology, 2019

'The Weight of a Shoe' was published by *Lunate*, 2021

The Message was published as a chapbook by Nightjar Press in 2018

PARTHIAN Short Stories

Figurehead
CARLY HOLMES
ISBN 978-1-912681-77-8
£10.00 • Paperback

'Through beautiful, rhythmic prose *Figurehead* weaves a sequence of stories that are strange, captivating, and unforgettable.' – Wales Arts Review

Whatever Happened to Rick Astley?
BRYONY RHEAM
ISBN: 978-1-914595-14-1
£10.00 • Paperback

'Bryony Rheam's short stories are skilled, perfectly formed, and compelling ... a deeply satisfying collection...'
– Karen Jennings

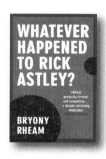

Local Fires
JOSHUA JONES
ISBN 978-1-913640-59-0
£10.00 • Paperback

'In this stunning series of interconnected tales, fires both literal and metaphorical blaze together to herald the emergence of a singular new Welsh literary voice.'

Men Alone
ÖZGÜR UYANIK
ISBN: 978-1-914595-82-0
£10.00 • Paperback

'This wry, moving, and beautifully crafted collection of stories is a rich and multilayered meditation on aloneness.'
– Tristan Hughes

PARTHIAN Fiction

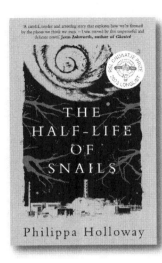

The Half-Life of Snails
PHILIPPA HOLLOWAY
ISBN 978-1-914595-52-3
£9.99 • Paperback

**Longlisted for
The RSL Ondaatje Prize 2023**

'A careful, tender and arresting story.' – Jenn Ashworth

The Lake
BIANCA BELLOVÁ
Translated by ALEX ZUCKER
ISBN 978-1-913640-52-1
£10.99 • Paperback

**Winner of
The EBRD Literature Prize**

**Winner of
The EU Prize For Literature**

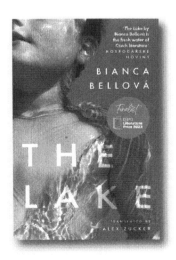

PARTHIAN Fiction

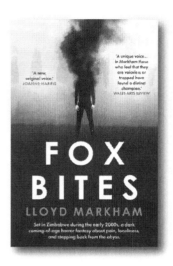

Fox Bites
LLOYD MARKHAM
ISBN 978-1-914595-17-2
£10.99 • Paperback

'A bold, ambitious new novel from Cardiff-based Lloyd Markham... a dark and genuinely gripping work of fantasy horror.'
– Joshua Rees

Unspeakable Beauty
GEORGIA CARYS WILLIAMS
ISBN 978-1-914595-42-4
£10.99 • Paperback

'A truly impressive achievement from a rising star of Welsh literature.'
– Gosia Buzzanca

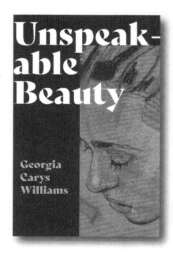